Inheriting Her Ghosts

by S.H. Cooper

Inheriting Her Ghosts

Published by Sleepless Sanctuary Publishing

This is a work of fiction. Names, characters, organizations, businesses, places, events and incidents either are the product of the author's imagination or are used fictitiously. Any resemblance to actual persons, living or dead, or actual events is entirely coincidental.

Cover by:
Morrighan Corbel

Edited by:
Elle Turpitt

Praise for
Inheriting Her Ghosts

"Gothic horror perfected. Atmospheric and moody from the first page, with a strongly drawn heroine, you'll want to read it by flickering candlelight during a storm. A sheer pleasure."

Laurel Hightower, author of *Crossroads*

"I don't think anything can prepare you for the way S.H. Cooper will drag you - kicking and screaming - into this dark, gothic story. Absolutely dripping with fright."

Steve Stred, author of *Ritual*

"A superbly atmospheric and beautifully written slice of Victorian gothic."

Beverley Lee, bestselling author of *The Ruin of Delicate Things*

For Ma and Dad,

who always let me be exactly who I am.

For Alex,

who knows all my ghosts and loves me anyway.

Table of Contents

Chapter One

The house inherited me as much as I did it. We were alike, this house and I. Both filled with bones that creaked and dark hallways where memories lingered still.

At forty-three, I was an oddity. By my matronly age, there were expectations, and I'd failed to meet them all. Truth be told, I'd never much cared for the male species. Or, more accurately, the human species as a whole. I was alone, and it suited me. But society cares not for the simple pleasures in which individuals indulge. If a person, particularly one of the fairer sex, does not fall into the status quo, then surely they must suffer from one malady or another. Were I a widow, my station would have been understandable, even lauded as respectable.

But alas, I had no dead husband on which to pin my solitary existence. It was merely by choice, and a woman's choice is a questionable thing indeed when it does not lead to marriage and procreation.

They went so far as to write about me in the papers. The wayward heiress of a socialite and a business tycoon who walled herself off behind her parents' fortune. While I did enjoy so many of the fanciful headlines they prescribed to me, I do believe my favourite will always be *The Curious Case of Eudora Fellowes*.

It does make me sound like such an interesting creature, doesn't it?

Had they known the truth of my situation, I fear their interest would have waned immediately. You see, I was never the lost soul they so imagined, nor did I drift between stacks of old papers and piled things. I simply preferred my own company and that of my loyal canines, who provided me with all of the fellowship I ever desired.

I resided in the city for many years, in the same home I had grown up in, bequeathed to me upon my dear mother's passing. Once she followed Papa in death, I released the few remaining staff still employed by the estate and was quite content to fill the rooms with my books and art instead of people. I also had my wolfhounds, Cerberus and Black Shuck. Despite their fearsome names and size, they were sweet, gentle beasts, and shared in my every activity.

Beyond being ideal consorts, they served a secondary purpose. A woman alone is thought to be easily approached. A woman in the company of a pair such as mine, who stood taller than many a man when on hind leg, is not so accessible. While I will not say for certain that I trained them to do so, if someone were so inclined to make my acquaintance, they were often met with a discouraging growl, which was enough to send them on their way.

Our lives, simple as they were, were uncomplicated and filled with more pleasant days than not.

I had thought I would remain in my family home for the remainder of my life. While it had never been my intention, per se, it did not seem a terrible fate for one such as myself. All of my needs were met and, while I did on frequent occasions miss my parents, I still felt something akin to their presence within those walls, and it did comfort me. Had I never received the letter informing me of my great-aunt's demise, I doubt I ever would have left at all.

When the knock came at the front door, causing my hounds to raise their heads, ears cocked curiously, I remained in my armchair. Rarely did I entertain guests, and only when they were expected. Were it one of my regular delivery men, dropping off the weekly groceries or other necessities, they knew to leave their goods on the back steps to be collected at my convenience. But given the late hour of the afternoon and their use of the incorrect entrance, I doubted very much it would be such a service. At the second sound of someone rapping against my door, I snapped the book I'd been reading shut and rose with some indignation. I commanded Cerberus and Black Shuck to remain in place and crossed through the parlour with unhurried steps, hoping my reluctance to respond might lead my visitor to abandon whatever duty had brought them to my home.

A third knock, more impatient still, indicated this was not to be.

I pulled the door open just enough to allow my head through and answered with all the hospitality I could muster, which is to say, a displeased frown and short, "Yes?"

The lad waiting outside looked up at me, owlish and impish at once beneath smudges of dirt. "Got post for you, marm."

"There is a letter slot, you know," I advised him, my eyes dropping pointedly toward the brass covered opening.

"Supposed to hand it to the lady of the house myself," he replied, puffing up with some deal of importance.

It was endearing to see one so young taking such pride in his task. I couldn't help but soften toward him. I stepped from behind the cover of the door and held out a hand to accept the paper-wrapped package tucked against his side. He studied it, then the remainder of me, with a suspicious furrowing of his brow.

“You’re the lady?”

“I am.”

“But you’ve got trousers on.”

“I do.”

This revelation as to my admittedly unusual style of dress perplexed him, and his dirtied fingers tightened ‘round the package while he inspected me with a narrowed gaze. Usually I would have put an end to such an open display of study, but I found his curiosity innocent despite its intensity. A child’s wonder at a changing world.

At last he relented and passed the package, creased from his handling, into my possession.

I remained in the entryway, watching him dash back down the steps and through the gate separating my property from the busy street beyond.

I returned to my armchair in the parlour and carefully unbound the twine holding the parchment together. Inside, a small collection of papers awaited me, topped by a letter addressed in an elegant hand to my name. It had come from a solicitor’s office, and for a moment I wondered if I had infringed upon someone’s good will.

To Mrs. E. Fellowes,

It is with the most sincere condolences that I write to inform you of your great-aunt, Mrs. Emmeline Parsings’, passing.

The name aroused faded images of an unsmiling face wreathed with pale hair. It was one I had not thought of in many years.

Our office has surmised that you are Mrs. Parsings’ next of kin and sole heir apparent.

It went on at length, delving at points into the complicated language of law I did not fully understand. What I did grasp, however, was that the entirety of her estate had been passed down to me. Included in the short list of assets was another name that surfaced half-remembered flashes from a distant childhood: High Hearth. Beside it, in smaller lettering, someone had added, “Residence”.

I sat back in my chair, the rest of the letter unread, and repeated the name aloud in a muted whisper. “High Hearth.”

It carried with it the ghostly shape of a great house, grey stone with tall, narrow windows staring out over a restless sea. I could envision myself, small beneath a wide brimmed hat, approaching a burgundy door, from the centre of which a brass gargoyle’s head clutching the knocker between its teeth snarled down at me. What lay beyond that door was lost behind the fog of age.

Of only one thing I was certain: the single visit to the place, and with the woman who resided within, had left a chill in place of memories.

I dismissed the lingering unease evoked by a childish perception and finished the letter, whereupon I was presented with a choice: take ownership of High Hearth and all of its belongings, or sell it and retain the proceeds. My written response was requested in as timely a fashion as I could manage.

I set the letter aside and eased back in my chair, my fingers steepled and pressed pensively to my lips while I considered the offer. Were I to turn it down, I would remain in my lifelong home, where I had established myself and wanted for nothing. Should I accept, I would be able to escape to the country, where I might enjoy peaceful respite in whatever years remained to me.

The following days were spent rereading the letter and carrying it from room to room while my dutiful hounds trailed close at my heels. I sat at my mother’s vanity in her powder room, left as it had been when she still had use of it, and sought her guidance as I had so often before when she still lived. I perched in the large leather chair behind my father's desk in his study, where the faint scent of pipe tobacco remained if I concentrated enough, and thoroughly weighed my options, just as he would have done when faced with some large decision.

Three days after I learned of my great-aunt's passing, I wrote to the solicitor to inform him I would take ownership of High Hearth.

The decision to leave my home did not come lightly. My very being ached at the thought of our parting. But I longed for time and space and distance that it could not grant me. There would never be silence outside its windows. No freedom from prying eyes and the gossiping hens that surrounded me. No escape from the curious case of Eudora Fellowes.

I left the city with no fanfare and only a pair of steamer trunks. No one would miss me, nor I them. Truly, I doubted very much that anyone would notice my absence at all until a new face appeared at the door of what had been the Fellowes family home.

I secured a train compartment for myself and my dogs, ensuring we would not be made to share with any other northbound souls, and the last I saw of the city was through a veil of fog beyond my seat's window. It faded behind us at a rapid rate, replaced by the rolling hills of the countryside beneath an iron sky. We ventured for some hours, passing through smaller cities and towns than from whence we came, until our eventual arrival at a station just south of our final destination.

I disembarked, Cereberus and Black Shuck's presence affording me a wide berth from other passengers, and was met upon the platform by one Mr. Crawford Bentley, my great-aunt's solicitor. Upon first glance, one might be led to believe he was little more than a moustache and spectacles beneath the brim of his tall hat, but a closer inspection would prove him to be a person of pleasing countenance.

"Mrs. Fellowes, I presume?" he said as he approached, hesitating only when Cerberus emitted a low rumble. "Hello, I am Mr. Bentley. I hope your journey thus far has been agreeable."

I laid a hand upon my dog's head, soothing him immediately, and nodded. "Eudora, if you please."

We kept our introductions brief while we waited for a porter to bring my luggage, then, in short order, were within a carriage that would carry us to High Hearth. I was happy to sit in the silence that had settled between us, listening only to the groan of the wheels and my dogs' panting breath, but the road made a conversationalist of Mr. Bentley.

"Your aunt has left you a fine inheritance," he said. It was a rather coarse statement, but those of the country persuasion often lacked the subtleties of the city, and I overlooked it. When I merely inclined my head in response, he continued. "In addition to the house, you are also heir to the small fortune she left behind. It is a tidy sum, coming to —"

Here, I stopped him. "I am sure whatever great-aunt Emmeline has seen fit to bestow upon me will be made available in her estate papers."

"Yes, but I thought —"

It took some gentle rebuking, but eventually the good solicitor realized his error and retreated back behind his moustache. I had never been one given to speaking so openly about such private matters, a condition instilled within me by my father, and was quite satisfied to wait until I could review the documents myself. To his credit, Mr. Bentley remained a silent participant for much of our journey, interrupting the quiet only to point out some feature he thought might interest me.

None did so much as the stone house rising on the horizon.

It was as I remembered it: intimidating, sturdy, beautiful. As we drew nearer, I became acutely aware of how the passage of time had aged it. The facade was more weathered than my memory allowed, the greenery crawling up its sides more prolific. The drive was untended and our carriage bounced sharply as it passed over the divots pockmarking its surface. Still, I hardly noticed.

As much as I would miss the house of my childhood, the moment I stepped beyond the threshold of High Hearth, I knew that I was home.

Chapter Two

The foyer fanned open, a dimly lit space made dimmer still by the layer of dust that had settled like a fine frost. Our driver deposited my trunks just inside and left with a tip of his flat cap. A wide staircase dominated one side of the room, and the other was cluttered with mismatched furniture and wooden crates overflowing with various gathered things. The hounds lifted their heads, nostrils flaring as they inhaled all the house had to offer. Black Shuck sneezed from tip to tail for his efforts and shook out his wiry coat. I stroked first his scruff then Cerberus' while I surveyed the congested hall.

"I do apologize for the state of things," Mr. Bentley said as he stepped into the doorway behind me. "By the time of your great-aunt's passing, she had become bedridden and much of the house has suffered for it."

"It would seem that it has been unoccupied," I replied into a swirl of tiny motes disturbed by our entrance. "Did she have anyone in her employ to care for her?"

"Well, it did take us time to locate you, Mrs. Fellowes." His words adopted a flustered edge. "Mrs. Bell would come from the village to clean house and cook and her son, Thomas, worked the grounds, but they were let go following her death. We could not continue paying their wages. Mrs. Parsings was laid to rest some months ago already and the residence has remained dormant while we searched for her next of kin. It was not within our authority to dispose of any of her belongings."

I merely nodded, not at all concerned with his reasoning or what had been left before me. I had never been one to shy away from soiled hands and sweat upon my brow. It would only help the place feel even more my own, having been tended back to a liveable condition through my efforts.

"Shall I show you to the dining room? I require your signature and there are things we will need to discuss before I depart," he asked.

"Please."

I followed Mr. Bentley through the narrow passage, mindful of my steps as we wove through my aunt's possessions. My dogs' claws clicked upon the wooden floor, close at my heels as always, but heads lowered with a wary curiosity at this new setting. As we delved deeper into High Hearth, it became apparent that the collection I had been greeted with extended far beyond the front door. I was loathe to call another person's property waste, but little of what I saw as we passed to the dining room appeared to be of any value or even usable in some cases. Clothing that seemed an ill-match for an elderly woman, toys that had no place in a childless home, broken and cobwebbed things half-hidden beneath carelessly thrown sheets.

The irony of the situation was not lost: it was the very home the curious public had curated for their idea of me.

The dining room had not been spared my great-aunt's tendencies. The sideboard table was buried beneath loose papers and hard-backed books. Crystal and silver had been allowed to become drab behind the glass panes of an imposing, dark wood hutch. Mr. Bentley busied himself with clearing a place for us at one end of the lengthy dining table.

"Have a seat, if you will." He had pulled a chair out and gestured in a gentlemanly fashion for me to take it.

I slid into it, and my hounds took their customary places to either side of me.

"The first matter at hand," Mr. Bentley said while seating himself at the head of the table with his briefcase, "is the property, both the house and all of the items within it. My office has prepared a deed, which I shall sign as executor, and it shall, all of it, be yours."

"And the things I do not wish to retain?" I asked, casting a wide glance that continued to catch new things I had not yet noticed.

"You may dispose of them as you see fit."

"How far is the village proper, Mr. Bentley?"

My sudden shift in topic caught him unawares and he sat, poised with fountain pen hovering over paper, while he considered my question. "By foot, almost three hours down the easterly road, give or take."

"I'd like to arrange for some of the locals to come and clear away that which I do not plan to keep. I trust your office can handle any payment as an expense of the estate?"

"Well, I can certainly make inquiries..." His pale eyes dropped to his papers. He shuffled them, unsigned, his moustache bristling over tightened lips.

"Is something the matter?"

Mr. Bentley set the papers down and smoothed them with apologetic thoroughness. His gaze remained furtive, darting back and forth, never quite meeting mine.

"Mr. Bentley?"

It was difficult to determine if his continued discomfort came from the topic at hand or from inexperience in facing such a direct line of questioning from a woman. I decided it did not matter and leaned forward with my elbows upon the table, my fingers threaded together beneath my chin while I awaited his answer.

"It is an unsavoury topic, Mrs. Fel—"

"Eudora."

He squirmed like an uncomfortable school boy dressed the part of solicitor.

"If you cannot be straightforward with me, Mr. Bentley, then I will have to assume this relationship simply will not work. I would request that you return to your office and send someone else in your place."

"I apologize, I do not wish to appear an unwilling participant in this matter," he said carefully.

"But?"

His fingers ceased their ticking and he exhaled brusquely. "I simply don't care to trouble you with the prattle of small minds."

"Forgive me if I ask you to elaborate."

The chair creaked beneath his weight as he shifted. Someone more consumed with societal graces might have released him from further interrogation at such signs of discomfort, but I was, much to his chagrin, not so polite.

He must have realized his performance was only stalling the conversation, not ending it as he had hoped, and he removed his spectacles to rub them vigorously with a handkerchief produced from his breast pocket.

"Your great-aunt was not a well-loved woman," he said as delicately as he was able.

"And now she is gone. I see no reason they should pass on whatever grudge they might possess to me."

"It is more complicated than a simple feud between neighbours. The rumours that surround this house, and Mrs. Parsings herself, are dark ones."

"It has already been a long day, Mr. Bentley. Please, speak freely and be done with it."

One corner of his moustache twitched. “If you insist.”

“I do.”

He sighed, a final display of reluctance. “I do hate to repeat such drivel, but...it has been said that your great-aunt was a practitioner of the black arts. That she communed with evil and tainted the very soil upon which High Hearth stands. There were reports of visiting mediums, of seances, and her own husband is believed to have gone missing. While no one can confirm the validity of these statements, the locals have, almost one and all, labelled her a witch, a murderess, or both.”

I failed in suppressing my amusement at such notions, earning a downward turn of Mr. Bentley’s mouth. “I have few memories of this place or my great-aunt,” I said, “but it was no secret that she suffered sombre moods after the death of her son.”

His eyebrows lifted slightly.

“You didn’t know about that?” I continued. “He was young, perhaps only ten. He became ill and never recovered. Likewise, Great-Aunt Emmaline didn’t either. My father attempted to maintain contact with her over the years, but she stopped responding after a time, and it became an exercise in futility. We did receive word once that her husband had been unable to accept the loss of their child and departed, but she did not know where he’d gone. It was one of the last things I remember Papa saying about her before they lost contact.”

“A more believable tale than what passes for fact in these parts,” Mr. Bentley said, eager to put the subject behind us. “And one I am more inclined to put my faith in. Be that as it may, I fear you will be hard pressed to call upon any of the young men from the village for help. I doubt any will set foot in this house.”

“What of the groundskeeper you mentioned before, Thomas? Would he come? Perhaps he has friends.”

"I don't rightly know. I've only spoken to them the once, to relieve them. I will say he seemed a..." here he hesitated to choose his word, "rough young man."

"I see. No matter. I will just have to find a less superstitious lot. Until then, I will do what I can as I can."

"I would hate to leave you with such a burden, Mrs. Fellowes."

And yet he did not follow up with any chivalrous offers of his own, which matched exactly my expectations for him. He was a quill man, made for niceties and formal occasions, but fluttered, feather-like, from actual labour. I did not think less of him for it. The world needs its quill men the same it does their harder counterparts. He relaxed in the face of my forgiving smile.

"I am not such a delicate thing," I said. "It will allow the house and I to become reacquainted."

"You are an interesting woman, Mrs. Fellowes, if you excuse my saying so."

"I have been called worse things."

He chuckled, once more reaching for his papers. "And I imagine it had little effect."

"Quite the contrary," I replied, amused. "If I had not been so reminded of my own peculiarities, perhaps I would have been able to forget them. Alas, we shall never know."

He shook his head, a gesture of good-natured befuddlement. "Alas indeed. Shall we carry on then?"

"Please."

Now returned to familiar territory, Mr. Bentley proceeded with renewed ease. Having learned of my distaste toward overly long financial conversations, he only briefly discussed the nature of the estate's assets, ensuring I understood what I now owned. He signed the property into my name and asked that I apply my own signature to a receipt stating I had accepted the entirety of my great-aunt's belongings in whatever condition they might be in and another form releasing Mr. Bentley and his office from any liability. Once done, he carefully folded the deed and sealed it with wax imprinted with the initials of his firm.

"I will retain the rest of the documents at my office for safekeeping and have Mrs. Parsings' accounts redrawn in your name. Once that's done, I will send you the details so you can access your inheritance. Until then, I took the liberty of stocking your larder with some essentials to get you started. Consider it part of my services. Do you have any questions or concerns?"

As I was about to decline, a sudden necessity sprang to the forefront of my mind. "If I could impose one more thing upon you, Mr. Bentley."

"Of course."

"Might you have a bicycle delivered here? It's possible there is one already hidden among my great-aunt's things, but based on what I've seen, I have no reason to think it would be in working order."

"A bicycle?"

"Yes. If I'm to make my way to town, I'd like the option to ride."

He twirled one corner of his moustache between his thumb and forefinger thoughtfully. "Yes, I do believe I can acquire one for you as early as the day after next."

"Wonderful. Whatever the cost, please add it to my bill."

"Is there anything else I can do for you? Provide a proper tour of the house, perhaps?"

"No, nothing I can think of."

"Well, if you do, I will leave you with my card. If you require anything additional, please feel free to send a telegram to my attention."

"Of course. Thank you for your assistance, Mr. Bentley. I can see why my great-aunt entrusted you with these matters."

As he pushed back from the table, poised for departure, he looked towards me once more, concern creasing his brow. "This is a large house, Mrs. Fellowes. You'll be alright on your own?"

"On my own?" I couldn't repress the smirk at such a suggestion and laid a hand on both of my dogs' heads. "I can assure you, I am never alone."

Mollified by my answer, he gathered his things, bid me a polite farewell, and turned down my invitation to walk him outside. His darting glance toward Black Shuck and Cerberus revealed it wasn't truly my company he was declining. I listened to his footsteps fade down the hall, then the click of the front door declaring his exit.

And then I was alone with my hounds in the belly of High Hearth.

Chapter Three

Once left to my own devices, it didn't take long for curiosity to start coursing through me. I removed my hat and tugged off my gloves, placing them on the table while bidding the dogs remain where they were, and set off to explore my new home. Their whining, soft and reluctant in their obedience, trailed after me in their stead.

The theme of abandonment continued throughout much of the main house. Having a housekeeper had done little to quell the tide of objects my great-aunt had seen fit to own, and each room was a testament to a need I didn't fully understand, an emptiness that refused to fill. Pathways had been carved out amidst the odds and ends to guide me from the dining room to the adjoining drawing room, where closed velvet curtains made for an oppressive atmosphere. From there, I progressed into the hall and followed it to the kitchen, presided over by a cast iron range. A door leading to the larder and pantry stood open on one side, another to the scullery and the servant's entrance across the way. It was with almost an unwilling voyeur's guilt that I peered into drawers and opened cabinetry, checking their stock.

True to Mr. Bentley's word, a small collection of basic goods to see me through my first few days at High Hearth huddled together on an otherwise bare pantry shelf.

Further venturing took me to the eastern wing of the house, where the fading light of the late afternoon barely reached. The growing dark seemed to swallow my footsteps as I made my way to a door, shut as if to keep out the encroaching shadows. Mindful that I'd soon need to make my way back to the kitchen, where I'd seen oil lamps, candles, and matches stowed within a cupboard, I closed my fingers 'round the knob.

It did not budge beneath my touch.

I stood before the locked door, pondering where a woman such as Emmeline Parsings might've kept its key, when a floorboard squeaked from inside the closed off room.

My grip tightened reflexively on the knob, expression pulled into tight uncertainty.

Another creak, so soft it was nearly imperceptible.

I arched forward, ear cocked toward the sound. Mice, I imagined, and no surprise, given how things had been allowed to deteriorate. As I stood there, consumed with listening for the scuffling of tiny feet, I became aware of an odour emanating from within. Dreamlike in its subtlety, a scent that clings long after its source has been extinguished. It was familiar, but lacked the comfort afforded by my father's preferred brand.

Pipe tobacco.

I considered it was perhaps remnant of Mr. Bentley's visit, but I had noticed no such odour upon his person whilst we'd shared the close quarters of the carriage, nor when we sat side by side at the table. Older then, left by a gentleman guest, or maybe even my great-uncle, although that seemed highly unlikely given the many years since he'd absconded into obscurity.

A study then, I surmised, or a business room in which the men of the house had gathered. No doubt closed off once there were no more of them to use it, now home to opportunistic rodents. An issue I would have to handle another day, for the longer I stood there, the deeper the darkness around me became. I pressed my ear to the door one more time, only to be met with complete silence, before feeling my way along the wall back to the kitchen.

The oil lamps proved useless, their stores having gone dry, but a brief search soon produced a candelabra, in which I placed a trio of long tiered candles. The orange glow of their flames was warm and welcome. With my lighting secured, I whistled for my pair and invited them to join me for an unceremonious supper of toasted bread, eggs, and sausage cooked on the stove. I'd been pleased to find the good solicitor had gone so far as to have the coal already waiting for me when I went to light it.

"We'll have something more appropriate once I've been to the village," I promised the dogs, although they were wholly content with their share.

The silence that settled over the house, now steeped in night, was incomplete and often interrupted. The distant, unyielding crash of surf upon shore rose over the cliffs. Wind knocked at every window and bellowed down the chimneys, to which High Hearth responded with low groans, protesting the drafts slipping through and chilling its interior.

I had thought I would find such things peaceful, even comforting, but after a life spent in the city, where nature gave way to man and domestic beast, these noises were alien to me. When I became aware of how close I was keeping to my candelabra, I scoffed, but did not separate from it. I was not one given to flights of fancy, seeing things born of shadow and strange sound, but neither was I immune to my imagination's whims when faced with the unfamiliar. I was sure, given some time to adjust, it would all fade into the background of my evenings.

Black Shuck whimpered at my feet.

"Oh, you poor beasts," I crooned, suddenly contrite for how negligent I'd been towards their needs. "Come, let's get you outside."

They sprang upright and, after I'd picked up the candelabra, followed me enthusiastically to the servant's entrance. The sliding bolt screeched as I pulled it and the door itself, swollen in its frame, required some persuasion before it swung open. At my nod, my pair bound past me, noses pressed to the ground. I remained in the doorway, a hand raised to protect the candles from the whipping wind.

From what little I could see from my vantage point, the back garden was overrun with spiralling vines turned brown by the changing season and bushes that had long since shed any kind of manicured shape. There was no footpath left, only swaths of flattened weeds to show where others had tread. I kept the hounds in my sight, unwilling to let them wander further before I had a chance to inspect the property more thoroughly, and called for them to return after they'd conducted their business.

I only began to wonder, after we were indoors once more with the rusted lock slid securely in place, who exactly had walked those bent and broken trails left in the garden of this long vacant house?

It was not a matter I allowed myself to dwell on. I was in the country now and likely shared my land with any number of vermin that might make an abandoned garden their home. Voles, perhaps, or the same family of mice that had burrowed into the study. Surely regular travel by even such small creatures would eventually leave its mark upon the earth. Yet another thing I would simply have to become accustomed to.

Dismissing any further concerns, I hastily washed the dinner dishes in the large basin sink and left them to dry in the scullery. After tucking a book of matches against my breast, I walked back down the hall, to the entryway where my luggage had been left upon on our arrival. Instead of hauling the two trunks up the steps, I put down the candelabra and opened the one I knew to be carrying my bedclothes.

A glint of silver caught the candlelight from within a muslin wrapping tucked protectively against the side of the trunk. I smiled, having forgotten I'd placed my parents' portraits with my clothing to keep them from becoming damaged during my travels, and took them out.

Papa had been resistant to the idea of photography when I first broached the topic, believing it to be a laborious affair wasted on the likes of him. Mother was a more enthusiastic participant and, in addition to helping me convince Papa, she took charge of finding a suitable photographer to capture them both. When the day had come, she took the utmost care with her appearance and selected Papa's suit, which she fretted over until he was seated in front of the camera.

While he had found his own portrait to be mediocre at best, he could hardly take his eyes from Mother's.

"It will do," he had said simply, but to see him gaze at it ever after, then to Mother herself, was to see him become besotted all over again.

To look upon them with such tender memory was bittersweet and I was not satisfied with simply replacing them in the trunk until a later time. As they had enjoyed a place of honour in our previous home, so would they here, and no better place was there than upon the parlour mantle.

After winding my way around heaps to place them, I went back to the trunk for my nightclothes and dressing gown and draped them over my arm. The corner of my latest sampler peeking out from beneath folded skirts caught my attention, and I plucked it and its twines of thread up as well, along with a book of poems from my second trunk. Should I not be able to sleep, as I much suspected would be the case, then I would be able to keep myself otherwise occupied. So armed to face my first night in this new place, I motioned for my hounds to take to the stairs before me and started up behind them.

The going was slow, brought on by a combination of the items balanced precariously in my arms, the effort to keep the candelabra aloft, and the troublesome hem of my travel costume. I'd thought it a lovely outfit when I dressed that morning, a smart wool gown in deepest brown with matching jacket, but now it had become a cumbersome thing, only serving to remind me why I so preferred the freedom of trousers. Cerberus and Black Shuck continued to the upper floor, oblivious to my hardship, and together vanished around the corner in search of new smells. I let them go. This was their home as much as mine now and I'd grant them the same independence here that they'd always known.

Halfway up the stairwell, the poetry book wiggled loose from my fingertip hold and tumbled to the floor, landing with pages splayed at my feet. I heaved a sigh, considered leaving it until morning, then shifted my clothing and sampler to a more amenable position to allow me to stoop and pick it up. I started to stand again, book reclaimed, when the most peculiar sensation washed over me.

The flesh along the back of my neck prickled sharply, and my breathing slowed of its own accord into shallow, shaking gasps. I stared straight ahead, shoulders drawn back, posture stiff as I straightened, a deer who'd just caught the scent of a hunter. Only it was no smell that had alerted me. No sound or flitting vision in the corner of my eye.

Just the unshakeable certainty that someone was standing behind me.

A step creaked in the dark.

My heart leapt, skipping its next beat, then raced in a thrumming patter that filled my ears. My limbs had become lead, weighted down by fear and the knowledge that no one else should have been in my residence, and I could not force myself to turn or run ahead. Even my voice failed me and I could not call for my hounds.

Not until the fingers closed on the back of my skirt.

"Cerberus! Black Shuck! To me!" I shouted.

The responding thunder of my dogs' rapid approach drowned out my heartbeat and emboldened me. I wrenched around, candelabra leading, my things spilling from my grasp, and turned to find empty black.

Confused, my chest heaving, I held the candelabra higher, but it revealed no figure slinking just out of view. The gloom of the entryway remained undisturbed. At the top of the stairs, Cerberus and Black Shuck observed me with untroubled eyes, their tails low, but wagging with a guarded air that asked for my reassurance. Certainly not the reaction I would have expected if there were an unwelcome party lurking.

Not yet satisfied, I patted my thigh, their signal to stay at my side, and gathered my skirt into a fist to charge down the steps. I swept from room to room, illuminating every corner, peering behind every piece of furniture, checking every lock.

But I found no menacing intruder.

No cowering prowler.

No one.

The house was, save for myself and my pair, empty.

Calmer now with my hounds so close and my search complete, I sank against a doorframe, a still excited titter escaping my lips.

"Forgive me, my darlings," I said, palm pressed to the base of my throat. "I did not mean to startle you."

They responded by sitting heavily upon their bottoms, tails sweeping back and forth across the hardwood floor. I stroked their heads in turn, glad that only they had been present for such foolishness. I'd always prided myself on being a rational woman, neither overly emotional or reactionary, but it would seem that such facades, no matter how carefully curated, could so quickly turn fragile.

"Imagine what they would say," I murmured to myself with some measure of humour, "those who think me some great and terrible mystery. To see me acting so, and all because of..." My words trailed off and I met Cerberus' steady gaze. "Because of what?"

Something had pulled upon my skirt, of that there was no denying, but I could not make sense of what it had been. A wayward draft, or, in my frightened state, could I have stepped upon the back of my own dress without realizing it? I chuckled at the notion, embarrassing in its plausibility, and continued to develop a list of equally likely scenarios.

I'd come up with nearly a dozen by the time I came and went from the kitchen, the cleaver from the butcher's block now in my possession.

Because for every harmless idea I conjured, another lingered like a shade thrown across the back of my thoughts. That there *had* been someone; someone I had not discovered who was now in a carefully chosen hiding spot, waiting until I could be caught unawares again.

It was such a silly conceit.

But if, by some sliver of a chance, it were true, and I was not as alone as I believed, they would find I was not some simple prey without tooth or claw.

And if they dared to lay a finger upon either of my hounds, they would learn just how hard I was willing to bite.

***

I selected the first bedroom at the top of the stairs as my own. Its smaller size and nearness to the main thoroughfare made it clear this was not the lady of the house's chamber, but it would suit my needs for the time being. After a moment's consideration, I wedged the small corner chair in front of the door.

"Do not think me absurd," I said aloud, more for my own benefit than for Black Shuck and Cerberus, who gave little indication they questioned my action at all. "It's merely a precaution to help me sleep."

Even by candlelight, I could see the grey settlement of dust upon every surface, including the quilted bedspread. The window slid open with little complaint and I shook each piece of bedding into the night air until they were of breathable quality again. With the bed remade, I sat upon the stool in front of a modest vanity and unpinned my hair, letting it unfurl from its neat coif down my back. Although still the rich colour of cherrywood, streaks of silver had appeared at my temples. I ran my forefinger delicately along these lighter strands, mesmerized, as I frequently was, by this obvious sign of age.

The beginning of the body's betrayal, at war with a heart and mind still wrapped in all the trappings of youth.

I smiled, a small expression, but one that deepened the lines around my eyes and mouth, and I wondered, not for the first time, if I had followed too closely my own path, diverging from the smoother courses laid so neatly at my feet by society and circumstance. I had no children to care for me in my elder years, no husband with whom to enjoy the twilight of my life. Would I regret it, when I was no longer able to leave my bed, with only my thoughts for company?

My smile widened, and the lines creased deeper still.

Such sentiments were as fleeting then as they had been in my twenties, when the topic of marriage had loomed over my life like a gallows. Aside from my dogs, I had always been my most treasured companion. Time could not take that from me, even as I shrank beneath its inevitable weight.

My mortality so faced, I changed into my nightdress, hung my travel costume in the wardrobe, its only occupant for the time being, and sat against the pillows, propped up by the brass bed frame. The cleaver sat atop my book beside me, and I took up my sampler, upon which was embroidered an unfinished pair of cardinals surrounded by an ivy border. I was quite pleased with how the birds were taking shape, and while the hounds circled and settled upon the rug at my feet, I rethreaded my needle and began my stitching anew.

Chapter Four

I wasted no time in getting started the next morning, eager to put all of the preceding strangeness quickly behind me. The task of clearing out High Hearth was a daunting one, and thinking of the house as a singular unit made it altogether overwhelming. Instead, I parsed it into individual rooms, and determined I would focus all of my efforts on only one at a time. Dressed for the toil ahead in a pair of poorly fitted trousers and a blouse that had been rendered unwearable in polite society by paint stains upon the sleeves, I laid out my plans over a strong cup of bitter coffee and plate of scrambled egg, the latter of which my pair shared with me. I would begin in the parlour, a most suitable spot as it was where I envisioned spending most of my mornings, taking in the early sun when it deigned to show its face. But what would I do with the refuse? Simply moving it from that room into a lesser used area would only suffice for so long.

"When Mr. Bentley returns with the bicycle, I will discuss with him hiring a cart." I nodded along with my words. "Send it into town, let the locals have their way with it, then discard the rest. As long as it is out of this...*my* house, I do not care where it ends up."

The hoard that awaited me was denser and more disorganized than I had imagined. My great-aunt's appetite for things, no matter how useless, had been voracious. Broken furniture, torn paintings, ornamental figurines missing limbs. Any real sense of personality or preference had been overrun by sheer mixed quantity. I made use of a long wicker basket I found pushed against a wall and filled it with the worst of the lot, the things I was sure no one would want. Kneeling beneath the piano revealed a stack of hat boxes of varying size. The smaller ones held bobbles and sewing supplies, but the contents of the larger captured my attention.

The frames were gilded ovals bordered by delicate carved wreaths. The first portrait I pulled out showed a young woman painted before a nondescript backing staring solemnly outward. Her pale hair and stern features had remained the same throughout her life, it would seem, for even though I'd only met her when she was older, I recognized her right away as my great-aunt. I laid her picture aside and took out the next. Another with a seated Emmeline, but this time she was joined by a tall man, severe in expression, with hair oiled back to curl behind his ears and a well-groomed beard. His hand rested on her shoulder. From their dress, fine Sunday fare, and the rose lying across my great-aunt's lap, it would seem to have been their wedding day.

The positioning was common enough, but I noted that she was turned inward, away from him, and instead of having her hands folded elegantly over one another, they were balled up and tucked against her midsection.

Closed and cold.

Their next family portrait included an infant, no more than a year old, held in Emmeline's lap. Given our family history, I knew this to be my father's unfortunate cousin. Here, he had the fat, round cheeks of a healthy, well-loved babe, which made his fate hardly ten years later seem that much crueller. She appeared to be holding the child close, fingers entwined around his middle with an affection she had lacked on her wedding day. Her husband stood proud at her side, a man made complete by wife and heir.

He was not touching her in this painting, but still she was angled away from his presence, a subtle posture, aligning him toward her back, one I might have missed had I not been studying it with such rapt attention. It appeared she had taken more to motherhood than matrimony.

I did not know the particulars of my great-aunt's marriage, but I was beginning to suspect it had not been a match made out of love. During one of our few conversations on the topic, Papa said she had wed later in life, well after his own parents had spoken their vows. Swept up while on the cusp of spinsterhood at the overly ripe age of thirty-one or two.

The final portrait I pulled from the box was taken in photograph. Its subject was a boy, no older than ten years, with lids half-hooded over vacant eyes. His suit was dark, as was the cloth hung behind him, and he was laid back against pillows with his arms folded over his stomach. Gone was the fullness of his cheeks, hollowed and pale, and his face was slack, free of expression. Across the bottom was written the name "Master Thaddeus F. Parsings".

While the frames of the previous pictures still retained some of their sheen, the gold leaf of this one had dulled considerably, and the detail of the ornamental foliage surrounding it had been smoothed away, signs of a repeated and regular handling. A mother's last link to her departed son.

With a great sense of care, I replaced most of the portraits in the hat box. These I would not dispose of. Although they held no real sentimental value for me, they were still documentation of a branch of the family tree I was not well acquainted with. Truly, I was grateful to my great-aunt for what she had left me, even if it had been an arrangement brought about by shared blood instead of direct intent, and it did not feel right to do away with the history that had brought me to High Hearth. The family portrait I displayed alongside the pair of Papa and Mother. But Thaddeus' memento mori felt altogether too personal. Too imbued with a private grief etched in fingerprints upon its surface.

Mr. Bentley stated my great-aunt had been laid to rest months before, most likely in a nearby cemetery. I would visit her, and leave with her this most precious keepsake.

By the time I finished, I had uncovered a sofa, its burgundy velvet seating outlined in dark wood, a handsomely ornate armchair and its simpler lady's chair counterpart, and a centre table to place them around. The small piano, in desperate need of tune and tending, still made for a fine accent piece in front of the three tall windows facing out over the lawn. I sat heavily upon the armchair, a seat usually reserved for the head of house and so appropriate for me and my position, and surveyed my work.

"It's starting to look serviceable, don't you think?" I asked over my shoulder to the hounds lying lengthwise across the doorway.

They rolled their eyes toward me, but did not raise their heads, so great was their indifference to my accomplishment.

"A fine celebratory pair you make," I scoffed, wiping my hands upon my trouser legs.

I could imagine us, a year from then, seated in that same room, paintings of serene landscapes hung upon the walls, a shelf of my favourite books for ease of access whenever I desired to revisit them, a plush rug to take some of the cold out of the floor. I would fill it with my things and myself, and it would be home. I allowed myself a satisfied grin that lasted until I stepped over the dogs, into the hall, and was met by the heap of things I had decided not to keep.

"I cannot just leave it here," I lamented, then, more quietly, wondered, "Can I?"

It was unsightly to be sure, but who would see it except for me? And even if someone else were to happen by and find me living in such a state, surely they could not too harshly judge a lone woman caught during a transient time.

Not, after what Mr. Bentley had told me, that there would be a great many people eager to offer their welcome.

With a shake of my head at the backward nature of High Hearth's reputation, I contained as much as I could into a single corner of the entryway and moved on to the next room, a library brimming with rows of books. The door opened to stale air and aged paper, and it was with no small measure of relief that I discovered very little stored within. This would not have been one of the rooms my great-aunt visited with any regularity, and so it must have remained closed and overlooked.

I threw back the brocade curtains, examined the nearest titles, many of them having to do with land ownership and financial decision making, and left it to ventilate. I did believe I would make great use of it once I replaced its current selection with one more to my liking. It would be a slow process, but one I would relish in.

The final room yet untouched in the eastern wing was the one barred behind the locked door. A cursory attempt at its knob proved that it had not, by some miracle, become unfastened overnight. I stared at it, pensively tapping my forefinger to my cheek before I thought better of it. After my exploits through so much dust and grime, I doubted very much that touching my face with unwashed hands was wise. Just thinking on it made my skin itch with a hundred tiny insect legs brought to life through the power of suggestion. More than that, I was suddenly acutely aware of the warm ache in my back and the growing stiffness in my knees. Hours of crawling about on the floor and carrying more than my usual weight had done me no favours.

"After only one room?" I admonished myself, then more gently added, "But what is my hurry? Neither the house or myself are going anywhere."

Instead of a race, I should view it as a leisurely stroll toward my goal. As much as I wanted it to be done, I was but a single person, and the house was so very large and so very full. I could be content with managing only a room a day, any less would be unforgivably lazy, and if I felt it in me to do more, so be it. But in that moment, after my long travel, restless night, and active morning, I deemed it acceptable that I retire for the remainder of the day.

The first order of business, now that my working hours were behind me, was to bathe.

Cerberus and Black Shuck proved as helpful in dragging my clothes trunk upstairs as they had been with cleaning, which is to say, not at all. They waited until I'd made it to the top of the steps before rising, stretching with languid slowness, and following at the pace of a pair of old maids. I unpacked my things, making neat piles upon my bed by article type, with the intention of hanging them later: gowns and dresses, blouses, trousers, and undergarments. I had, after some consideration, even brought two corsets, one ribbon and the other bone. As disagreeable as I found them, there might still be occasions where I'd have to play the part of a tamed lady.

With my dressing gown in hand, I walked down the hall to draw a bath.

I did not use the bathing room within my great-aunt's chambers, opting instead for the smaller one unconnected to any bedroom. Truth be told, I hadn't gone into her suite at all since my arrival. Beyond the briefest of glances within, to a room veiled in gloom, I maintained my distance. Not from any feelings of foreboding, but rather as a matter of propriety. This had been her most intimate space, where she was both her most free and private self. Although I was already coming to fast terms with my ownership of High Hearth, there was a degree of separation in the more common areas of the house that made the process more palatable. Just as I had preserved my parents' personal quarters, pieces of me felt compelled to offer the same courtesy to Emmeline. The difference now was that the most tender nostalgia that had stayed my hands before no longer tethered me.

Until such time as I felt more firmly rooted within High Hearth, however, it would not be of terribly great importance to me.

I sank into the steaming waters of the claw foot tub, my eyes closed beneath a warm cloth. My joints loosened, coaxed into relaxing by the soothing heat, and I allowed myself to drift into a state of relaxation I had not known since receiving Mr. Bentley's initial correspondence.

It was shattered abruptly by an unexpected growl.

My pair were situated beside the tub, sitting on hind quarters with twin stares pointed toward the half-closed door. Their hackles were raised and ears pinned to skull, a phenomenon I had only encountered in them once or twice before. Black Shuck drew back his lips, baring gleaming fangs, as Cerberus rumbled again, the distant sound of thunder warning of an encroaching storm. I sat upright, draping an arm over the porcelain side to stroke their backs. Muscles rippled tensely beneath my touch, but did not ease as was so often the case.

"Easy, my sweetlings," I whispered, but still they did not soften. On the contrary, their growls deepened into snarls I did not recognize, their heads lowered near to the floor, nostrils flaring, and for the first time I saw them as they had been truly bred, as creatures made for the hunt.

It did not worry me for my sake, but for whomever, or whatever, was causing their distress.

With the hounds firmly planted between me and the door, I sprang upright and snatched my dressing gown around my body. How I regretted returning the cleaver to its place upon the butcher's block! The bathroom, small at it was with we three in it, offered no such form of protection.

Black Shuck lunged forward, jaws snapping at threat unseen, but he refrained from going further than the doorway, ever my faithful and obedient pet even in the midst of his fury. Likewise, Cerberus stood at his side, and to look upon them was to know the face of hellhounds waiting to be unleashed.

Trembling from the mingled chill of air and fright, I stepped from the bath, dressing gown clutched tight against me. Stillness permeated the hallway, lit with steel grey afternoon light, and the doors to the unused bedrooms remained closed, just as I had left them. There had been no footsteps or creaking of hinges to alert me of another.

And yet, a growing unease blossomed within my chest. As if, by some primitive instinct, I knew something waited beyond that bathroom.

As if I could feel the house itself holding its breath.

"Make yourself known," I demanded over my pair's harsh warning. "Or I will set my hounds upon you!"

Cerberus and Black Shuck bayed madly into the empty hall, rearing and tossing their heads, and each howl struck hammer-hard against my heart.

Something's coming.

It was not a conscious thought, but a certainty, cold and solid as ice. Eyes and reason warred with this knowledge that had dug its claws into my bones and raked them to the marrow.

Something's coming!

I yelled for my dogs to heel, sending them immediately to their rumps, and threw myself at the door, slamming it beneath my weight, and twisted its lock. I shrank what little distance I could away and dropped onto the closed toilet lid, unable to tear my gaze from the door.

How long we remained in the bathroom, shivering and shaking, taking what comfort we could in our nearness, I cannot say. It wasn't until the hounds rested their heads upon my lap, tongues lolling and tails swishing, returned once more to their genial natures, that I could bring myself to rise. Listening against the door produced only silence, and opening it the tiniest sliver showed an undisturbed hall, now swathed in amber hues from the setting sun. I crept forth, gown grasped tight at my neck and waist, dogs close behind.

The feeling from before, that certainty, had faded into an embarrassed befuddlement. The dogs must have alerted to something I had not heard and their response, so sudden and violent, had stirred in me a whirlwind of irrational fear. Just as I'd scared myself the night before.

It was the size and newness of High Hearth playing upon my mind, nothing more.

It was a calming reassurance, one I might have been able to nurse into true believability.

But when I reached my room, my stomach dropped, stone-like.

Every item of clothing was thrown into disarray, scattered about the floor, vanity, and stool.

But none had been so attacked as my corsets, left, boning twisted and broken, ribbons shredded, in the centre of my bed.

Chapter Five

I braced myself against the nearest surface, my knees suddenly too brittle to bear me upright. No longer could I tell myself it was merely rodents sharing my space or that I had given myself over to fanciful wonderings. This was an intentional act. A warning, perhaps? But by and from whom? And where were they hidden that even Cerberus and Black Shuck took no notice of them?

I tore through the house with renewed fervour, throwing back every curtain and leaving no wardrobe or cupboard closed, no matter how small. I continued well into the evening, when I was forced to fetch the candelabra to see by. I crept along on all fours, shining my light beneath beds and, when that revealed no hidden person, I struggled to lift the mattress corners to ensure no one could have crawled under or within. Not even my great-aunt's quarters escaped my scouring, for there were a great many places within, behind chaise lounges and among racks of gowns, where someone might conceal themselves. No matter how unlikely a course seemed, I took to it with a wild abandon.

At the end of it, all I had to show for my search was a dirtied dressing gown and scuffed knees.

I lowered myself on to the bottom step, thoughts reeling and heart racing. Twice now I had gone to great lengths to ensure my solitude, and twice I had confirmed it. If I did not have a room thrown into chaos upstairs, I might have suspected I was going mad. No matter how I tried to view my current situation through a logical lens, always did I circle back to the most basic, undeniable facts: my clothes had not scattered themselves across the room. Whalebone had not snapped of its own accord!

And yet there simply could not have been anyone else in High Hearth. I had combed through every last room with a thoroughness that rivalled even the hounds when they believed there was still some morsel of supper left uneaten.

No.

No, that was not true at all, was it.

There was one room I had not yet visited, not been in at all, fastened as it was to keep me out.

But for every lock, there must be a key, and now my whole purpose was dedicated to finding it.

Even in her ailing years, Emmeline had been the mistress of the house, and as such she would have kept in her possession a ring of keys granting her access to any and every part of her home. Mother had also carried one, although it bore far fewer instruments upon it than Emmeline's surely would, given the difference between the Fellowes city dwelling and this seaside manor. Always would I hear the gentle clinking of small metals and think of Mother, the brass ring worn at her hip announcing her approach. When not on her person, she had stored it in her vanity, and so it was to my great-aunt's chamber I hurried.

Jewellery, brushes, and combs crowded the vanity tabletop, and more of the same filled the drawers in uneven piles, catching them in their tracks and fighting against their opening. I wrested them free and clawed through them, unmindful of the old powder jars and lavender water vials tumbling over their sides. The third drawer I pulled from its place altogether and spilled at my feet, but no keys landed amongst the pile of tangled necklaces and mateless earrings. Leaving the mess, I turned to a side table, then another, tipping it in my mounting frustration.

The crash of wood ringing against the floor helped return me to my senses and I halted my tirade. I smoothed the front of my dressing gown in time with my breathing, urging myself to keep a clear head about me.

There's nothing so valuable as the ability to think during troubled times.

A family mantra often impressed upon me in my youth, I used the words as a balm to quell the panicked heat that had taken light in my chest.

Think.

Emmeline had been elderly and so unwell she'd been unable to leave her bed by Mr. Bentley's account. I had approached this quandary as if she were living the life of a healthier woman, still preparing for and ending her days seated before her mirror. But that would not have been the case.

I turned on my heel and strode with grim purpose to her bed.

It was wooden framed, its four posters rising like guardian spears at each corner. A bedspread of red and gold had been made up over plump pillows, the central of which retained a rounded concavity, as if awaiting its owner's return. The illusion was dashed when I ripped away the duvet and disrupted the pillow arrangement, feeling around beneath them with both arms buried to the elbow. I was beginning to despair, thinking this to be another fruitless search after not immediately coming upon my quarry, when my fingers brushed something cool and hard wedged between the headboard and mattress. A joyous cry leapt from my lips as I came away with a silver ring weighed down by at least a dozen keys.

With my bounty clutched close to my bosom, I returned once more to the ground floor and the door that so vexed me. One key, two, three, but none turned the latch, and I grit my teeth, urging the next and the next to do so.

Neither luck nor the appropriate key were with me.

My temper got the best of me and I flung the keyring. Its clattering against the wall brought the hounds to uncertain attention, their ears pricked forward. I stepped back, studying the door, made of heavy oak or walnut, and knew immediately it was not one I'd be able to force my way through unassisted. If I did not have the aid of a stronger party than I or the proper key to go through it, a different tool would have to suffice.

An axe, perhaps.

Having had a groundskeeper in employ indicated there would be a tool shed somewhere on the property, but it was growing too dark to venture out. I did not know the land, and given its unkempt state, I was more likely to injure myself than find what I was looking for. I bit my lip, looking to the windows of the entryway then back to the door. I did not relish the thought of another night spent ignorant as to what lay behind it, but I saw little other option. Arriving by foot to the village at some obscenely late hour, especially not knowing what kind of lodging I might find, would do little to endear me to its inhabitants. That did not mean I had to go about staying in a foolhardy manner.

I stacked high the things I had taken from the parlour in front of the door, placing those most breakable items on the outer edges. Should anyone open the door from inside, it would make contact with my tenuous tower and the chipped china and cracked porcelain would make quite the racket smashing upon the ground. I would not be able to miss it.

I escorted the hounds into the back garden, allowing them to stretch their legs under my careful watch, then made a supper of salt-dried pork and cheese laid on a slab of bread. As ever, Cerberus and Black Shuck were enthusiastic meal-time companions, but I took little pleasure in the food, barely tasting it as my attention focused anywhere and everywhere else. Mournful winds took on malicious undertones, the flickering candlelight cast sinister shadows. I left my place at the counter to repeatedly pace from window to window, back to the doorway looking into the hall, unable to settle.

I doubted I would find rest that night.

It was with great reluctance that I finally retired to my room, cleaver in hand, where still my clothes lay as if victims of a child's tantrum. I shut the door firmly behind us, once more dragging the vanity stool in front of it. The clothes I collected in a haphazard way and dropped them into my trunk, aware my carelessness would cost me hours at the iron. The corsets I merely pushed to the floor, unsalvageable as they were. Attempts at maintaining my routine were mechanical, interrupted by backwards glances slipping toward the door.

Disrobe. Redress. Remove hairpins. Brush.

Unsteady fingers made for poor embroidery and the words of my poetry book ran together in lines of illegible black. I pinched the bridge of my nose between my forefinger and thumb, weary in a way I had not been since the loss of my parents. It was not grief that plagued me now, but it ran deep all the same: a sense of utter aloneness. Helplessness. How silly it seemed, to compare the most tragic events of my life to this, but I knew no other way to explain it to myself. Doubt crept as shadow into my consciousness, bringing with it whispers of regret. Only a day within High Hearth and already I wondered if I had made a mistake, leaving the security of my family home for this alien one. My arrival had been so full of optimism and a sense of belongingness, that this was where I was meant to be.

Had I truly been so wrong?

No, I told myself, letting my book fall closed. It was only the musings of an exhausted mind fraught with fear. Whatever was happening, I would not only withstand it, but overcome it. I just had to figure out what *it* was.

In the meantime, trying to sleep was of paramount importance. I needed a clear and ready head if I were to make sense of my surroundings. I bid Black Shuck and Cerberus, curled on the rug at the foot of my bed, a good night and blew out the candles. Moonlight streamed in silver through the window, just enough to see how the dark distorted shapes and transformed the familiar. I pulled my quilt to my chin and turned on to my side with a huff. How close I felt to being a little girl cowering beneath her blankets once again. It would have been an amusing thought, had I been somewhere else, far and away.

There is something to be said for the body's ability to fall asleep even when the mind insists it is impossible. It did take some time after I closed my eyes, but the restless night I'd feared did not come to pass. I slumbered until mid-morning, far past what I was accustomed to, and would have for longer still, except that something I could not immediately identify roused me. I sighed into my pillow, not yet willing to crawl from the warm and comfortable cocoon I'd created around myself.

Weight shifted in the bed beside me.

"That had better not be you, Cerberus," I said, voice muffled by covered down. "You know better."

At the sound of his name, nails clicked across the floor and a cold nose brushed my forehead. I opened my eyes to a pair of shaggy faces staring back at me. Cerberus nuzzled me again, delighted at my waking.

The mattress dipped at my back, the weight rolling closer.

I yanked myself away in a quilted tangle that nearly sent me toppling over the mattress' edge. In my mad flurry I thought, for just an instant, I caught sight of dark hair over my shoulder.

But when I righted myself and turned more completely, the bed beside me lay vacant.

I sat rigidly, sheets held like a shield against my body, until I was brave enough to reach out and run a hand over the bedding to check it was truly unoccupied. The quilt was cold where I touched it, and I pulled back in mild shock. It had no right to be so cold! When I could bring myself to feel the area again, already the chill was dissipating.

I had thought a fair few things since High Hearth started to reveal itself to me, from rodent infestation to stowaway, always attempting to assign some realism to perceived oddities. I could call this a dream, perhaps, except I was very certain of my wakefulness, and prescribe a draft to the spot upon my quilt, except I had felt no such breeze when I laid my hand upon it. My pride, upbringing, and education urged me to accept such answers, false as they might ring, for doing so would keep me in the realm of reason. Never before had I strayed, thinking that those who did were gullible, content to accept even the most outlandish solutions if it meant their minds could remain idle, untroubled by more complex thought.

Yet, there I sat in the light of morning, bright and new, drawn toward a single word balanced on the edge of a precipice, beckoning me to follow it down.

Haunted.

Chapter Six

Haunted.

My logical soul recoiled at the mere thought, but I could not deny the growing foothold it was taking within me. How else to explain the veritable storm that had raged through my room and dashed my things to the floor? All without me ever hearing a sound. There was also the disturbing matter of the hounds' odd behaviour when I could see no cause for it.

Yet they had not reacted so moments before, when I was certain something shared my bed.

My attempts to make sense of my current circumstance only served to confound me further. There was still a chance, slim as it might've been, that a more tangible explanation would present itself, and it was to such a possibility I desperately clung, a lifeline to keep me on my feet while the ground felt as if it were turning to shifting sand beneath them.

It was that fragile tether that led me back to my previous plan, concocted in the throes of frustration, but one that granted me a goal, something to focus my fast-fraying attentions on.

I needed to open that door.

I redressed quickly in the soiled clothing from the previous day and haphazardly twisted and pinned my hair up, not a thought given to style or neatness. I selected my oldest pair of boots, low heeled and unpolished black leather, and laced them with short, determined rugs. Together with the dogs, I descended to the ground floor and passed through the hall, to the kitchen and out the servant's entrance.

The groundskeeper's shed was often tucked in some far corner of the property, kept out of sight so the family was not faced with such indecencies as manual labour, and I meant to find it.

Behind the house was a tangle of choking vines and weeds that had smothered anything planted with real intent. I stomped in a way most unladylike through the brambles, my trousers catching on nettles and thorns, passing a stone fountain that had once been the centrepiece of the garden. Thick, green water, ripe with stagnation, had collected at its bottom. The cherubic figure poised in its middle stared skyward, features obscured by mossy growth.

It gave his eyes such a plaintive appearance, as if begging the heavens for release before he was entirely consumed.

I pushed onward, seeking out some semblance of a path that might make my going easier, but any laid gravel had given way to nature's reclamation. My pair romped alongside me, traversing the snarled grounds with playful ease and bobbing between the bare skeletons of shrubbery. I envied their carefree frolicking as much as the sight of it lightened the burden weighing upon my heart, however briefly.

Beneath a crumbling lattice arch, salt air had eaten through a bench, rusting the wrought line of fleur-de-lis that decorated its back. Beyond that, a gazebo encircled by flowerbeds, dry and barren as recently dug graves, stared out toward the sea. The wind beat upon my face there, its whistle turned to a howl with my nearness. All that separated me from the grey abyss was a waist-high iron fence. A row of the spearheaded finials along its top had bent in one spot, and I shuddered to think of falling against that fence, and of what might happen if it didn't hold.

At last, as far back as the garden spread before it dropped into cliff face, I found the shed.

A small, narrow structure with a pitched roof, it had certainly seen better days, and when I shouldered open its door, it was into a cloud of gossamer webbing. I brushed it quickly from my person, praying I did not come away with a new eight-legged companion, and surveyed the murky outlines laid against the walls. The light that pierced the brackish coating of the shed's only window was hardly enough to see by, and I shuffled forward, squinting. The smell of mildew and dirt hung heavy, mixed with the faint trace of manure. The last groundskeeper, Thomas if I remembered rightly, did not appear to have been a fastidious man, and had left the tools strewn haphazardly about. I stepped over the handle of a hoe and skirted a shovel, standing upright with nose buried in the packed earth floor.

The axe hung from a hook beside an intimidating pair of gardening shears on the back wall. I stretched over the wheelbarrow sitting in front of it and braced myself for the pull of its weight as I tugged it down.

It came off the hook with a noisy scrape that was answered by a bark from outside.

Cautious at first, then more forceful, soon joined by his brother's voice, until both hounds were baying. I rushed from the shed, axe held low in a two-handed grip, to find them pacing at the fence, the same place with the misshapen finials. As I approached, a flutter of movement beyond the iron bars drew my eye. Something pale, there for a moment then gone, slipping over the edge of the cliff.

No sooner had it gone than the dogs reverted to a less agitated disposition, although they continued to sniff and paw along the bottom of the fence.

"Nothing more," I muttered, a plea to the Lord above and High Hearth itself for a moment's respite, and slapped my thigh to bring Cerberus and Black Shuck to my side. "Not right now."

I did not look back as we crossed through the garden on our return journey to the house. Even when all the small hairs on the back of my neck rose as one and my steps quickened of their own accord. Even as my skin pricked into goosebumps. Even as I passed beneath the melancholic cherub and his upturned gaze and I felt, with no uncertainty, something watching me from behind. My pair all but confirmed my suspicions when they slowed with anxious growls, heads starting to turn 'round, until I snapped for them to continue onward, into the house. They listened with unhappy whines. I leapt over the threshold in the same manner a child might jump into bed to avoid the monsters lurking underneath and fastened the deadbolt with a trembling exhale.

I remained in place, eyes closed, long enough to recollect my scattered wits, then I hefted my axe, its weight reminding me of my purpose, and made for the locked door.

I commanded the hounds to sit far and away from where I'd be working, concerned my inexperience might lend itself to injury. I'd be able to forgive myself should I fall victim to the axe's sharp edge, but not if it were one of my pair. After knocking aside the tower I'd previously erected, I took a wide legged stance, both hands curled around the handle, and chewed my lower lip. Ignorance birthed hesitancy and I stood poised to swing, but uncertain of how effective it might be. The axe had grown heavier here than it had been in the shed, I was convinced, and its head began to droop downward while I questioned whether this truly was the wisest course.

"Shh!"

Up shot the axe again, spurred into activity by the soft warning for silence that had come from behind the door. I did not stop to consider whether it might have been a trick of the ear or create a list of worldly things it could have been. Things I would have preferred it to be. The time for that was past me now. I swung, but not hard enough for the edge to bite into the wood, so I repositioned and brought it down again. It found purchase that time and I wrenched it free, chopping over and over, but for all my whole-bodied efforts, I made little progress against the hearty surface.

The first knock rang in time with the axe's fall.

I stopped, the blade embedded in the door, and stared down the hall to the entryway. The drumming of the gargoyle's brass knocker echoed through the house again. Trepidation coiled in the pit of my stomach, constricting further when Black Shuck and Cerberus rumbled from the backs of their throats. I silenced them with an upheld hand.

A third knock, this one louder than the last.

I left the axe hanging from where I'd last made contact, like a grotesque warning of my impending return, and, on near tiptoe, approached the front door.

"Mr. Bentley?" I called without opening it, hopeful it was only the solicitor making good on his promise to return with a bicycle.

"No," a deep voice answered with an apologetic quality, "but it is by his bidding that I'm here. I'm Matthew Kenzie; vicar of the village parish. I had hoped to introduce myself to the new lady of High Hearth."

Never had I been so relieved to hear another person! I flung open the door to a tall man in a black wool suit, from the neck of which peeked a white collar. By the faint lines on his face, he appeared to be of a similar age to me. Behind him, a horse and hooded gig, its top drawn up over the two-seater cart to ward off any inclement weather, waited in the drive.

Whatever he expected of the new lady of High Hearth, his expression made it clear it was not me. He was unable to stop the telling widening of his eyes, although he did his best to correct his features in short order. I could not blame him for such a reaction, I knew I must look a proper mess, but that was far from my most pressing concern.

"You're…" he started.

"Eudora Fellowes," my introduction was rushed and breathless. "Please, come in." It was not a stranger's company I was eager for, but for someone to witness the house as I was, in all of its eccentricities. And who better to deal with matters of spiritualism than a man of God? It truly felt fortuitous that he would appear as I faced such uncharted challenges.

He lingered just outside the vestibule. "Is everything alright, Mrs. Fellowes?"

I shoved back a stray curl that had escaped its pin and met his gaze. "I'm really beginning to think it's not. In fact, I'm inclined to say the opposite: Something is very wrong here."

Well-practiced concern creased his brow and he stepped inside, removing his bowler hat as he did so to reveal a hairless head thrown almost out of balance by his thick beard. "Whatever is the matter?"

While the worry stamped openly upon him was honest, it did not perfectly conceal the less benevolent opinions I so easily recognized. How accustomed I had become to them. The subtle scrutiny of my wardrobe, always pointed down the tip of their nose, the indignant straightening of lapels when I did not turn my stare demurely downward. Mr. Kenzie kept his discomfort smaller still, settling for turning his hat in his hands, but it read loudly to me nonetheless. Had we been in more normal times, it would have been enough to make me laugh, this nervous twitch brought on by nothing more than unkempt hair and the visible existence of a woman's legs. Certainly, I would have dismissed him back to his gig and delighted in his going, for I was not one to tolerate being made a spectacle in my own home.

Instead, quite against my usual inclinations, I said, "This way, I'll show you."

My pair sat tall and stiff, immobile save for their dark eyes following the vicar as he followed me. He started slightly at the sight of them, his footsteps faltering.

"Pay them no mind," I said, unable to take pleasure in his surprise. "It's here, this door. I've been—"

"Is that an axe?"

"Yes," I said, attempting to disregard its importance with a brief explanation. "I need to get in this room, but cannot find the key. There's—"

"Your solution, then, was to...cut it down?"

I pinched my lips into a tight line to hold back the temper flaring higher with each interruption. "Yes. Because something is in there!"

"Something?" he asked, beguiled. "Why not summon a locksmith? Surely that would have been preferable to," he paused to gesture toward the scarred door with his hat, "this."

"I fear I don't have time to wait for one. And after what Mr. Bentley told me about the regards with which High Hearth is held in the village—"

Mr. Kenzie tutted sympathetically, once more driving me to exasperated silence. "I am well aware of Mrs. Parsings' reputation, and how it soured the view of the house. It's partly why I came, you see. To begin the healing process."

"Be that as it may, I—"

"You need not worry, Mrs. Fellowes. We will bring you into the fold, and you will see you do not need to attend to such matters by yourself."

My patience spent, I snapped, "You're not listening to me. I am *not* alone!"

"Oh." His brows rose. "Forgive me, I was under the impression you had taken residence by yourself." Craning his neck with some hopefulness, he asked, "Is your husband available?"

"I am unwed," I said, toes curling in my boots with my efforts to remain civil. "Please, Vicar, listen to me. There is something, or perhaps even some*one*, in High Hearth with me. Since almost the moment of my arrival, I have been plagued by...strangeness. Feelings and—"

"My good woman," he spoke with the maddening calm of a parent soothing a nightmare. "I am sure this has all been very overwhelming. Learning of your loss, coming here, to such a large house. Of course you've been unsettled." He grew more comfortable as he spoke, a man of the pulpit used to letting his words carry him. He cast another disparaging look toward the axe, then turned. "I believe we passed the parlour on our way in, did we not? Let us sit and talk awhile."

I almost rejected the offer outright, too incensed at his slights for conversation, but he had already left me, inviting himself into the parlour as if I myself had extended the welcome. The hounds cocked their heads, sensing my ire, but I did not call upon them to join me and so they stayed while I pursued the vicar. I found him standing before the mantle, studying the photograph of my great-aunt and uncle on their wedding day.

"Emmeline Parsings," he said softly. "She was a divisive figure, wasn't she? Were you and she close?"

"No," I replied, and when my curiosity won out over my annoyance, I asked, "Did you know her?"

"I'm afraid not. She did not attend church and, when I attempted to visit her here, I was turned away. My predecessor, Vicar Whitley, did, however. To some degree, anyway. She was a member of the parish then, after he married her to her husband, and then had the unfortunate duty of performing last rites over her son." He made the sign of the cross before the portrait and took a seat upon the sofa. "That's when all this nasty business began, in her grief. She was never seen in church again after."

I slid into the armchair. "Nasty business?"

"Yes. The talk of her turning away from God in her hour of need and summoning darkness in His stead. Truly deplorable claims that should not be made without absolute certainty. But I'm afraid once people start talking, they are slow to stop. If ever there had been a chance for her to return, it was taken by such vile nattering."

"Granted," he continued, and I noticed it was with none of the reluctance someone unused to gossip might possess, "she had always been a queer one, your great-aunt, or so it's said. She was already matronly by the time Mr. Parsings took her hand and brought her here. You'd think a woman of her standing and age would have been eager to rebuild a new social circle, but by all accounts, she was a poor hostess and infrequent guest."

"Perhaps her's was not a socialite's calling," I said dryly, at which Mr. Kenzie chuckled.

"An option, to be sure, but one that defies the very nature of women, don't you agree?" He did not wait for me to answer. "Mind you, this is all second-hand knowledge, mostly gathered from my predecessor and elders who were familiar, or as familiar as one could be, with Mrs. Parsings. They ascribed it to a life lived in the city, where the sexes mix too freely and forget propriety. Whatever the reason, it's a shame she never found her place here."

My teeth had set into the edges of my tongue at his tone, at once full of pity and patronizing. I decided to steer him away from further discussion by returning him to the immediate matter for both our sakes. "Yes, a shame. But my aunt aside, Vicar, I'd very much like to continue our previous conversation about what I've been experiencing."

He frowned slightly, then brightened with understanding. "Ah, the sensation that you're not alone?"

"Yes. I've only been here a matter of days, but already I've encountered a number of things I cannot explain."

"Such as?"

"My clothes being strewn about my room. Hands pressed to the small of my back when no one is there. Someone—"

Mr. Kenzie leaned forward, elbows resting upon his knees and hands clasped in front of him. "I couldn't help but notice your dogs out in the hall."

"Cerberus and Black Shuck."

"If those are their names, then yes. They are large, aren't they? Large enough to make a mess of things or press against your back, wouldn't you say?"

"If you're implying my pair are responsible for the things that have gone on here, I am afraid you are sorely mistaken," I said, bridling at the suggestion.

"Even the best trained pets sometimes get up to misadventure—"

"You misunderstand me. It could not have been them because they've hardly left my side."

There it was again, that smile meant to assure me he knew best. How I wished to take that hat from his hands and smash it over his face so I didn't have to see it!

"Much has happened lately, and given your fragility—"

"I beg your pardon?"

"My apologies at any offense taken, Mrs. Fellowes, I meant only that you've been placed under a great deal of stress and made to handle matters more suited for a husband. It's not expected that a woman should be made to shoulder all of this herself."

"That is entirely irrelevant!" Heat rose in my cheeks and I resented my body for so transparently showcasing my emotions.

"There is no need to raise your voice, Mrs. Fellowes."

"Perhaps if I do, you will finally hear me!"

"You are becoming hysterical," he said sharply.

I clamped my mouth shut to withhold the torrent of abuse threatening to spew from me. There were few, if any, words that I hated more than "hysterical". So much could be swept aside when that single word was prescribed. Righteous anger reduced to nothing more than an inability to control one's moods. Had I not been so at a loss with the goings on in High Hearth, I would have demanded he remove himself immediately from my presence.

He pulled at his beard in exaggerated strokes. "Lets the both of us take a moment to calm ourselves," he said. "I believe tea would be helpful. Would you be so kind?"

I stood with a stiff nod and left the parlour, my blood burning in my veins. I had attended church back home, having grown up in my parents' parish, but the older I'd gotten, the more personal I'd felt my connection to God. I continued to read my Bible and recite my prayers, but on terms dictated by no one other than myself. It would seem that trend would continue.

"Come," I said to my pair as I stalked by on my way to the kitchen, where I stoked a fire in the oven and set a kettle on the stove top to boil.

I pet the hounds' heads, muttering to them about our guest while I waited for the water to heat.

From the quiet, a piercing shriek suddenly ripped through the house, loud enough to shake the windows in their panes and rattle the cutlery in its drawers, as if a banshee had descended. I dropped to the floor, arms thrown around both of the dogs' heads to block their ears from the worst of it. They leaned into me, shaking terribly, tails dropped between their legs, and I could scarcely withhold my own terrified scream. It dragged on, shrill and painful, driving the three of us to huddle against the cupboards. My ears throbbed with the sound.

And then it ended, abrupt as it began, with the slamming of a door.

I scrambled upright. "Mr. Kenzie?" I yelled, to no answer. Stumbling at an uneven gait on jellied legs, I retraced my steps back to the parlour, this time accompanied by Cerberus and Black Shuck.

Save for the black bowler hat he'd carried in with him, left lying on the floor, there was no sign of the vicar. I called for him again, but again received no response, so I made for the front door and yanked it open.

The vicar's gig was speeding down the drive as quickly as the horse could pull it, leaving me once more on my own in High Hearth.

Chapter Seven

I watched the fleeing gig until it had turned to a speck on the horizon. Until the dust kicked up by the horse's mad flight had resettled upon the road. I stood there, affixed within the entryway as firmly as the gargoyle knocker was upon the door, and I watched the house, and me with it, become enveloped once more in a shroud of hushed stillness. Such solitude, so complete that it made an outside world seem impossibly beyond my grasp. Like I was some tiny insect trapped within a glass and, were I to try and escape, I would only hurl myself against the deceptively clear barrier.

Never gaining ground.

Never getting out.

It was ridiculous, bordering on *hysterical*, to entertain this idea of absolute isolation. Of course I could leash the hounds and take to the road, walking the long miles to the village, where I would indeed find the life and people that seemed lost to me. But what then? Where had I to go, once my welcome was worn through, but right back here?

My vision clouded with tears that ran in hot trails down my cheeks. I had not realized, for all the displeasure he'd caused me, how much hope I'd managed to place in Mr. Kenzie in such a short time. That he might dispel whatever claimed the shadows of High Hearth and bring peace in the Lord's name, blessing it so that I might live on, undisturbed. Clearly mine had been a misplaced faith in a man of weak constitution.

Save for my loyal dogs, I truly was alone.

But, I reminded myself, fingers knotted tightly as if to hold my very person together, hadn't that always been my preferred state? Outside of my late parents, I'd never sought company nor advice from others. Every trouble I'd faced had been my own to solve, in my own time, in my own way. From rebuffing ingenuine suitors who thought having my hand might be advantageous to stepping between belligerent carriage drivers and the horses suffering under the overeager whips they threatened to turn on me, I had not shied away, even when I could scarcely speak or stand upright from fear.

I would do well to remember who, at her core, Eudora Fellowes was.

Turning to face the vestibule again was an act of staring down a lion's open jaws. Except then, at least, I would have seen the fangs and known its nature. Hunter, predator, but not cruel. The animal kingdom was unapologetic in its gruesome straightforwardness. This was something else entirely. A hidden thing with motives I could not begin to guess at.

Always had my first response to the unknown been to seek out a better understanding of it. Thus far, I had gone about doing so in a way that defied my own nature, attempting brute force and acts of violence in place of a more learned approach. In my desperate fright, I'd forgone applying thought in troubled times, focusing instead on the tangible task of getting the door open. That would still come in time, for there remained my gut instinct that something important lay on the other side.

But first, I resolved to educate myself.

I was not well-versed in hauntings beyond the stories told around the fire on Christmas Eve, but I doubted those seasonal tales would be of much help. I required a more scholarly approach, something that would explain outright what I might expect and how I could put an end to it. I steeled my nerves to re-enter the house and made first for the kitchen, where I removed the singing kettle from the stovetop, then the library, calling for my pair as I did so. They fell in ready step behind me and, as always, I drew strength from their steadfast and solid presence.

As unlikely as it was that my great-uncle owned any texts that might suit my needs, perhaps my great-aunt, in her rumoured curiosity, had procured some and scattered them where they would go unnoticed, camouflaged by their more respectable fellows.

I skimmed the fabric-bound books, my fingers sliding over embossed spines that referred to matters of the mundane. After the first row, I began pulling them out, one by one, and flipping through them as if I might find mystical passages or arcane secrets hidden between their pages.

One stack of displaced books turned to two, turned to three, until I had all but cleared out the shelves. Had I an interest in banking or gentleman's etiquette decades out of date, it would have been a valuable find, but among them were no works pertaining to the occult.

I sat heavily upon a footstool, my head in my hands, and my entire body heaved with an expelled sigh. Black Shuck's nose appeared between my knees, nudging for attention, and Cerberus sought to squeeze his large head in the crook of my arm, snuffling loudly as he was wont to do when concerned. I unfolded myself and took hold of both of their faces in turn, scratching their cheeks and chins while telling them all would be well.

I could only hope I was not betraying the trust that shone so bright in their eyes by speaking hasty untruths.

It was that same trust, pure and unquestioning, that stirred in me a slow anger. These huge beasts, so capable of defending themselves, looked to me for consolation, for reassurance, for answers to all things that unsettled them. I was Mother. Their great protector. And there was no role I cherished or would guard more fiercely. That something would dare terrorize my pair, no matter the source, was unconscionable. When I had brought them home two years prior, following shortly after my mother's funeral, I had made a promise to them: I would care for them completely until the end of their days.

I meant it even more now than I had then.

Pushing myself up, spurred by this maternal heat, I marched past them, into the hall, and shouted to the rafters.

"If truly I am haunted, then make yourself known, spectre! What do you want? Tell me what keeps you here?" My words vanished among the dreck surrounding me and I released a loud cry after them, furious and frustrated by my powerlessness.

High Hearth held its confidence and the sea breezes wheezed through its cracks like faint, taunting laughter.

***

With little else to do but ponder my next step, I tore the axe from the door and carried it with me to the kitchen. Its usefulness was in serious question, but I could not deny there was a certain comfort in keeping it close.

While my thoughts churned, as if caught in the dizzying currents of a whirlpool, I reheated the kettle and prepared a small lunch from my dwindling supplies. I sipped the tea slowly, letting the warmth wash down my throat and spread through my chest, and I stared out the window, searching the slate skies for any kind of answer.

"What am I to do?" I whispered over the rim of my cup.

My resolve remained, but the path forward was layered in so much black I had no way to know whether I was making progress or in what direction I should go next. I could dig for years amongst my aunt's mountains of things and never find anything of use. Even applying the previous pattern I'd used to locate her keyring did not seem applicable for I had no experience upon which to base where one might hide their illicit materials.

"Give me something," I pleaded aloud, although to whom it was directed, not even I was sure. "Help me."

It was a listless request to an unyielding void and I exhaled shortly through my nose at having spoken at all.

Hysterical, indeed.

I left my dishes sitting, still dirty, on the counter, and trudged with axe and hounds to the parlour, where the vicar's bowler lay beside the sofa. Cerberus gave it a cursory sniff, then backed rapidly away with a shake of his head, turning toward his brother as if to warn him against repeating his action. I stooped and picked it up, setting it on the centre table until such time the vicar returned for it or I could bring it to him. The hounds continued to eye it with twitching noses.

"He was an unpleasant sort, wasn't he?" I asked them as lightly as I was able, curling up in the armchair with my legs tucked beneath me. The moment could have passed for normal if one were to overlook the weapon propped up at my side. "Don't fret, my darlings, I don't believe we'll be made to host any more of his visits."

Once they had relaxed enough to lay down, I closed my eyes, willing away the images of snapped corsets, the observed feelings, the echoes of an unearthly scream and a voice from inside a locked room, and I searched for some shred of peace within myself that I might wrap around my heart to better fortify it against whatever was yet to come.

Chapter Eight

It came as if from a dream, and indeed, I first thought I had drifted off, the closing of my eyes an invitation for weariness to overtake me. But even upon their opening, it continued, floating down the staircase, faint as a whisper.

Huna blentyn ar fy mynwes,
Clyd a chynnes ydyw hon;
Breichiau mam sy'n dyn am danat,
Cariad mam sy dan fy mron…

I had to concentrate to make sure I truly was hearing it and, after a short period, there was no denying what it was: A child's voice, singing sweet and slow, but muffled, from somewhere on the floor above.

My fingernails bit into the arms of the chair, but otherwise I was rigid, a statue built of trepidation. Without rising, the hounds turned toward the sound, but provided no further reaction, as if this was some common occurrence they had no reason to trouble themselves over. Dumbfounded by their apathy, I peeled myself from the chair, took up the axe resting against it, and moved to stand in the parlour's doorway. The song continued and I strained to make sense of the lyrics, all but lost in the distance between the singer and myself.

A glance back to my pair showed them in the same unconcerned repose. Always had I trusted in their intuition regarding persons or situations, and always had I found them to be sound, but in this instance I could not help but doubt in their calm assessment.

Shuffling to the bottom of the staircase, fighting every instinct for every inch, I laid a hand on the bannister and tilted my ear toward the voice.

Ni cha dim amharu'th gyntun,
Ni wna undyn â thi gam;
Huna'n dawel, anwyl blentyn,
Huna'n fwyn ar fron dy fam.

The first step groaned noisily under my weight and I froze, expecting the singing to cease at the pronouncement of my ascent. It continued however, as if the child either did not hear my approach, or simply did not care.

At the landing, I paused again, this time to more accurately locate where it was coming from, and followed it to the room across from my great-aunt's suite.

Huna'n dawel heno, huna,
Huna'n fwyn, y tlws ei lun;
Pam yr wyt yn awr yn gwenu,
Gwenu'n dirion yn dy hun?

Closer, the words took on a veneer of familiarity, but only in cadence and pronunciation, not understanding. As a girl, I'd been nannied by a woman with a curious accent, and likewise a neighbouring child with whom I'd been made to socialize had had one of the same. While we were at play, the two would often converse softly in their mother tongue, a lilting speech with poetic peaks and valleys.

I had not heard it since Mother reprimanded her for its use in front of me after I, in my ignorance of prejudice, said I wished to speak in that fairy language.

"Welsh?"

That quickly became a secondary thought as I stared at the door, nostrils flaring with nervous, erratic breath.

I knew I had left it closed, yet now it stood a sliver open.

My lips moved soundlessly with the Lord's Prayer and it was only through my surety in its divine protection that I was able to move forward. Little by little, I nudged the opening wider with the toe of my boot, until I stood fully in its entrance. The curtains were drawn, as they had been when I conducted my searches, and the dark filled every nook and cranny. As with so much of the house, this room too was filled with things old, forgotten, and useless.

Amongst them, though, was a motif more apparent than elsewhere. A baffling collection of dolls, their porcelain skin spiderwebbed with cracks, dresses of silk and lace styled for a child, tea sets, zoetropes, and automata toys, all with girlish frills and flair. They had been pushed to the sides, made to make room for more of her horde, but their prevalence could not be overlooked. What use had my great-aunt had for these? She was a gatherer of indiscriminate things to be sure, but these were themed so specifically, and all in one room, that I was made to ponder why a woman who had only ever birthed a son might have them.

And still the child sang, their voice drifting out from under the great bed at its centre.

Ai angylion fry sy'n gwenu
Arnat ti yn gwenu'n llon?
Tithau'n gwenu'n ôl dan huno,
Huno'n dawel ar fy mron.

It never grew in volume or changed its languid pace, but I foundered all the same, slipping back a few steps until I was pressed against the wall opposite the room. The doorway yawned, a cavernous maw waiting to close around me, and the grip I kept on the axe's handle whitened my knuckles. My eyes squeezed shut, and I willed myself to believe I had, in fact, fallen asleep in the parlour and this was just a dream, a nightmare, and I need only wake for it to end.

A heavy weight, too substantial for a mere figment, brushed against my side.

The scream that came from me was short and strangled. Instead of swinging the axe, I hugged it closer and jumped away, and it was only when I realized what had touched me that I was glad for my ineffectiveness.

Black Shuck wagged his tail, blissfully unaware of how close he'd tread to tragedy. At the sight of him, I broke into a gasping, relieved mix of laughter and tears and sank to my knees. The axe slid from weakened fingers and fell to the floor, where I left it for the time being, having come to accept it made me more a danger to myself and my pair than anything else that might have been in High Hearth. I wrapped my arms around Black Shuck's neck, and looked past him for his brother, never far.

"Cerberus!"

I lurched to my feet, but he had already bypassed me and was well into the room, his nose pressed to the ground against the dust ruffle that concealed the underside of the bed. He whined softly, lowering himself into a bow, and swiped at something behind the ruffle. I shrieked his name a second time, plagued immediately by visions of him being dragged behind that lace curtain, and ran toward him, but so intent was he on whatever he'd found, I went unheeded. By the time I reached him, he had twisted his head so that it would fit under the bed and he was growling.

But it was not an angry sound.

I knew my dogs' noises the way a mother knows her baby's cries. This was not the warning of a hound on the verge of attack. It was a summons, a request for play, the same he used to stir Black Shuck into more puckish moods. Cerberus snorted and whined again, an extended trill into the shadows, while his tail waved wildly back and forth in the air. His brother would have joined him, but I commanded him to stay where he was, unwilling to put both at risk. Much to his displeasure, I hauled Cerberus out by his haunches, no easy feat, and dragged him into the hall, where I collapsed between my pair.

And it was only then, once I was sitting back on my heels and gazing into the room, that I realized the singing had stopped. It had, it occurred to me, the moment Cerberus began his investigation.

I looked to him, tongue lolling, completely at ease, if a bit disgruntled by my rough treatment, then to Black Shuck, who mirrored his unbothered pose, and I found my terror turning to timid bewilderment.

If something in that room posed a danger to me, it would not have been met by gentle giants. I had seen evidence enough of that already.

It was on quivering legs that I finally convinced myself to re-enter the room and went directly to the window to pull back the curtains. Overcast light flooded in, chasing the gloom into the far corners. I lingered there, my heart still skipping, and took many a deep breath before I could make myself kneel at the bedside previously occupied by Cerberus.

I hesitated once more, the ruffles' edge pinched between finger and thumb, and bit my lip before yanking it upward.

No creeping horror awaited me, only more stored bits and pieces. One object in particular had been disturbed so that it sat at an angle in the forefront, apart from the rest. Whether this was by Cerberus' efforts or something else, I didn't wish to dwell, but its odd positioning drew me to it. I did not believe it was by mere coincidence it had been left so. It was so close, I hardly had to reach for it at all, and tugged it easily out into the open.

A layer of dust coated the mahogany jewellery casket, dulling the painted flowers across its top and front. A gold latch held its domed lid to its rectangular body. Part of me, probably the reasonable part, resisted the idea of lifting that latch and viewing its contents, like it might unlock so much more than just this box and I had not the nerve for it. But I could not continue to live so, cloaked in fear and constant wonder.

I flicked it upward and tilted back the lid.

Folded letters, ten or so of them, filled the casket, their edges curled and dried with age. I leafed through them, most careful in my handling, until I reached the bottom of the stack, and selected the one with the earliest date in its corner, some forty years before. With delicate precision, I spread it out over my lap to unveil clumsy script written in a heavy hand that did not match the eloquence of its words.

To Mrs. Emmeline Parsings,

It is with such great sorrow that the news of your son's death has reached me. Although we two are strangers, I know well the unfathomable pain born from such loss, for I too have had a child reclaimed unto God's Kingdom. I write to you as a kindred spirit, and with an offer of hope that you shan't find anywhere else. I know how you can speak with Master Thaddeus again.

The name at the end was signed with such an overabundance of flourish as to be unreadable.

The correspondence disgusted me in two parts: firstly, the bold claim, bordering on the profane, stating the author could commune with the dead, and secondly, more loathsome still, making such a claim to a grieving mother. To what end, I could not fathom from this single letter, but it left a curdled taste at the back of my throat.

I am not sure of what I was first aware, the chill that had settled over the room, turning my breath to white fog, or the hounds' rancour vibrating from deep within their chests. I looked up from the paper to find them with hackles raised, their weight shifting between paws as they grappled with my command to remain at the doorway.

"No," I ordered them, albeit the word quavered, and I clambered to my knees. "Stay!"

The letters were shoved back into the casket far less graciously than I'd removed them, and I stood with it held tight against my body. The cold swept across me as if carried by an arctic wind and my steps were fumbling and slow. A loud splintering cut through the room, then a shatter. One of the dolls fell from its shelf, its head reduced to small shards. The cracks in the one that had been seated beside it spread like thin veins across its face before it, too, burst, as if crushed by a great force. The destruction carried on down the line of dolls, until each slumped upon the shelf or lay on the floor below it, headless.

Each porcelain fracture was accompanied by the stifled sobs of a child beneath the bed.

I staggered forward to the cacophony of breaking and anguish, the icy air robbing me of my scream. My pair jumped forward to meet me and I took hold of Black Shuck's scruff. My stiff fingers curled within his coat and, like a rope thrown to a drowning man at sea, I clung to him and used his warmth and stability to hurl myself into the hall.

As soon as I crossed the threshold, the door slammed at my back and all descended into silence, save for the echoes of a young girl weeping.

Chapter Nine

If there were a sanctuary from the entities that haunted High Hearth, I had not the first clue where to find it. So, as a child would, I retreated with my hounds to my room, where I locked us in behind a weak barricade of trunks and chair. I watched the knob, casket still grasped close between my arms, and expected at any moment it would begin to turn.

My pair remained at alert, stalking restlessly from my side, seated at the edge of my bed, to the door, where they pressed their noses to its edges.

Strained seconds ticked by into minutes, and it was only with the dogs' eventual placidity that I was able to also relax, albeit to a most superficial degree. I sagged, shoulders drooping and my chin tilting toward my chest, and I could hardly make myself do more than gaze down at the jewellery casket in my lap until my thoughts untangled themselves.

With growing calm and clarity, I regarded the casket more shrewdly. I had asked for answers, and in return, something had wanted me to find this.

I could not ignore so obvious a sign in my favour.

Sitting back on folded legs, I reopened the lid and took all the letters out to spread them across the quilt, lining them up so they read from oldest correspondence to the latest dated of the bunch. Included with them was a poster.

The vividness of its colours had faded into muddied hues, but still the painted image of the girl at its centre was clear. Dark haired and adorned in the black garb of mourning far too old for her youthful features, she sat with hands outstretched, palms facing upwards. Her face was likewise tilted up, large eyes opened wide and beseeching. Above her, blocky text proclaimed, *The Valley Witch: Guide to the Spirit Realm*, and smaller lettering below her read, *Seances, 12 shillings*.

As to how this came to be part of the casket's contents became clear upon turning my attention to the letters.

It would seem by the repeated requests for my great-aunt's response, dated one and two months following the letter I'd already read, that she was not at first enticed by the author's promises, which were expounded upon in each additional missive. One of them made reference to the poster, which they'd sent with the belief it might add some credibility to their story.

The girl exhibited on it was called Morwen, I learned, and it was through her that the dead spoke. Despite being only twelve years of age, she was already exhibiting great control over her gifts, through which she had come to know Thaddeus, or so said the writer.

Then came the fourth letter, in which it was stated Master Thaddeus had made it known he missed Jenny. This appeared to have been a trigger for Emmeline, for the next letter was an elated reply at finally having received word from her. Her answer must have been steeped in scepticism, for what came next were many additional details regarding the boy: favoured foods, names of loved ones, places he might have visited.

Often is Morwen possessed by the spirits of the departed, but rarely so thoroughly as has been the case with young Thaddeus. He is eager to return home.

And so my great-aunt must have been convinced of the girl's authenticity, because the remaining letters, each with increasing brevity, spoke of how Morwen might come to High Hearth. The last had only a handful of lines, scribbled with none of the care taken in its predecessors.

I, of course, will accompany my charge. We require funds to travel such a distance. If you can provide for our passage, we can arrive before the month's end.

The lack of additional correspondence indicated Emmeline had sent the money. If this had been the case, and Morwen and her guardian had come to the manor, then it meant I had a name for the singing child who had acted as my guide to this box.

More grimly, given my experiences, it also lent itself to the idea she had then never left.

Questions surged like ocean waves, but none roared so as loud as, "What happened to her?" Had there been an accident? Might she have fallen ill, as Thaddeus had? Or perhaps the author of those letters, who I had come to think of as more a handler than parental figure, had harmed her. But why?

No further details presented themselves upon additional read-throughs, and I found myself gazing into the painted face of the poster's child, studying the flatly drawn eyes, the mature grieving gown, her dark hair.

Dark hair.

Flashes of that morning, already so long ago, crossed my mind, when I had turned to catch a glimpse of just such a thing upon waking to the belief someone had been sharing my bed.

"Morwen," I murmured softly, fingertips tracing her muted features.

She had been trying to communicate with me. The surety with which I now felt her needfulness came as a surprise and I pressed a hand flat against my chest, trying to catch my breath as if I'd been doused in icy water. No more could I deny her, hiding behind fear and closed doors.

"Morwen," I said again with added conviction. "If truly you are here, tell me how I might help you pass on, for I do not know what you need of me!"

A floorboard creaked in the hall.

When my pair did not alight with aggression, I moved forward, pushing aside my barrier, and stepped out. The light of day was fading and the hall had grown thick with shadow. I hesitated, searching the murk for signs of the girl, but the evening was a subdued one.

"Morwen?" I ventured to call, voice scratching with taut nerves.

There came a slamming from within my great-aunt's quarters, like the dropping of a heavy book upon the floor.

"No more will I hear that name!" a man's voice proclaimed heatedly.

I shrank into the doorframe, ready to take refuge again. The hounds rumbled softly, not quite growls, but the beginnings of such.

Footsteps reverberated toward me, and although the door did not open, there came the squeak of fast swinging hinges, then a pause in the steps.

"Thaddeus is gone." The ethereal voice, bound to no one, hitched, and a palpable pain filled the vacancy where a person should have been standing. "There is no changing that, by our efforts or anyone else's."

The footsteps carried on at an angry pace down the stairs. With a backwards glance to my hounds, who likewise looked to me for direction, I scuttled across to the bannister and gazed down, but the swelling gloom revealed nothing.

Black Shuck and Cerberus flanked me in tight formation as I descended.

Whatever we pursued, it did not bear the same intensity as previous encounters. It lacked the solidity of the creature I'd come to think of Morwen or the weighted presence that roused such passionate fear in me. I could not say exactly why, but I perceived this to be more nebulous and non-threatening, an echo instead of an active event. And perhaps that's what it was: a memory. A point in time so potent that it had come to be part of High Hearth's very structure.

That ever I would think such a thing, and more so that I could accept it as plausible, would have been laughable only days before.

Fretful though I was, I followed the sounds as I would an orator reciting a story.

The footsteps led me through the servant's entrance and into the garden. Slashes of weak light still cut through the clouds, but they would be short-lived as evening closed its fist over the land. Here, with heightened wariness, I bade my hounds to sit and stay and pressed further into the garden alone, trailing after the crunch of steps upon a gravel path that no longer existed.

They ended at the fence, in front of the spot with the bent finials.

Reserved sniffs turned to quiet sobs, then to low, mournful moans that stretched and grew, punctuated by bereaved repetitions of, "My boy. My boy."

Never had I heard a man sound so wounded, as if his very soul had fissured and erupted with volcanic agony. His howls were joined by my pair from their spot outside the servant's entrance, and their chilling chorus swirled into the oncoming winds.

The flurry of footfall that came up behind me was so sudden and quick I hardly had time to react at all.

I managed to twist my body, arms raised defensively in front of me, but the act was an unnecessary one. Instead the steps, driven by force unseen, flew past me, and the lamentations ended in a startled grunt. Metal strained beneath sudden weight. The man's voice started to say something, its inflection rising in disbelieving question, but again he was cut off, this time by a woman's furious snarl.

His scream was short, ending in a grunt of exertion.

"Help me," the disembodied voice pleaded from the lip of the cliff, and so desperate was the call that I found myself moving to the fence before I could remind myself no one was truly there. "Please...I can't hold on." He shuddered and boots kicked without purchase against rock face, sending a shower of loose pebbles raining down. "You cannot leave me here! Please! Em—!"

He struggled with a fervid vigour, and I was paralyzed, helpless but to listen to this man's final moments play out with increasing panic, until with a harrowing shout, it ended.

At that, I could no longer contain myself and leaned across the finials, fingers wrapped tight around the warped spearheads. The waves fell hard against the crags, spraying foam across the jagged rocks, rising at a knifepoint through the surface.

And in the midst of the frothing roil, there was movement.

Driftwood, I assumed, pushed toward an unyielding shoreline by the current. But it twisted, bent, and it was only when it started to pull itself upward I realized my initial impression had been wrong. It was no stray log I'd seen bobbing in the water, but a human arm, stretched to an unnatural length. A bloated face, colourless as fish belly, half eaten by time and sea creature, broke through the tide, and I was struck by a terrible sense of recognition.

Once the thing, for I was loathe to name it man, had hauled itself completely free of the water, the tattered remains of a suit still clinging to its distended form, it began to scale the cliff, skittering crab-like and quick, pulling itself up and up and up on its long arms.

As it climbed, swollen eyes, glazed as marbles, turned toward me, and it hissed.

"*Emmeliiiine.*"

Closer it drew, carrying with it a decayed, salty stench, and I flung myself away from the fence to retrace my steps through the garden at a run. The hounds bayed and I pinned all my focus on their raised voices and returning to them.

The fence groaned behind me, protesting the monstrous beast heaving itself over its top. I looked back to see him crawling after me on all fours, elongated arms granting him a spider's grace.

"*Emmeliiiine.*"

My pair had abandoned their post and were charging toward me, fangs on full display, but I screamed, "Inside, inside!"

Cerberus resisted longer than his brother, having caught sight of the creature bearing down on us, and his bark was a dire warning that did nothing to slow the drowned man.

"*Emmeliiiine.*"

Skidding to a stop, I shouted harshly for Cerberus, to which he finally responded with grudging obedience, although it was not without more thunderous barking to keep our pursuer at bay.

Still, on he came.

Black Shuck was first inside, and I ushered a belligerent Cerberus after him, before finally following myself. The latch screeched into place and I leaned heavily upon the door, waiting for it to quake beneath the ghastly man's attempts to enter. I listened to his scuffling just on the other side, which drove the dogs into a near frenzy, but he did not throw himself upon it.

His nails scraped softly over the door's wood.

"*Emmeliiiine.*"

There followed a sibilant hiss, then a shambling retreat.

As soon as I no longer heard the dreadful thing lurking outside, I went immediately to the cupboard for a candle and, once lit, sprinted to the parlour.

The first portrait on the mantle was my dear mother's, the second my father's, and the sight of their faces mingled with my absolute terror came as a thousand tiny pin pricks across my heart. What I would have given for a single second of their company, to feel their warmth and know their support again. What light just the sound of their voices would have shed upon this hell in which I'd found myself. I maintained contact with Mother's eyes, drawing what little solace I could from her image, then shifted away, toward the reason I had come.

My great-aunt's family portrait was the last in the mantle's line, and I held my candle close to it so the flame washed it in flickering orange. There was my great-aunt, sitting with her doomed child, and standing beside them, was *him*.

I had not wanted to believe it, but now, so facing his painted likeness, I could not deny it. His features had become gruesomely disfigured, his arms lengthened and disproportionate, as if stretched by countless nights spent dangling over the cliff's edge, but I knew him.

My great-uncle.

And through him, I was starting to know my great-aunt better as well.

Chapter Ten

I coaxed a fire into life within the hearth and pushed the armchair close. The ball into which I tucked myself was small and tight with a nightmare's dread that slithered through my blood and encircled my bones. I pressed my fists against my eyes and let prayers fall in a murmured flurry from my lips. Only when Black Shuck laid his head upon the arm of my chair was I able to unfurl, but even then just enough to reach for him. Cerberus lay beside me, head raised and ears lifted, listening.

High Hearth breathed in muted whispers, its cracks and crevices dolefully inhaling the sea air. Night made a labyrinth of the house and it seemed to build itself further in shadow. Rooms doubled in the dark, hallways pressed in and pointed on, longer than they had before. It was a restless place in a way I had not known a building could be; unsatisfied, hungry, the very air thick with its disquiet.

And as it grew, I could feel myself shrinking, if not in body, then in mind and spirit, becoming a mouse scurrying from hole to hole while the cat hunted. Had it not been for my pair, and that I sat beneath the watchful gaze of my late parents, I fear I might have disappeared altogether in that chair, consumed by High Hearth and its secrets.

I shut my eyes again, endeavouring to drive the house from my head with the feel of the fire's heat and the weight of Black Shuck's chin upon my knees. Things I knew to be real.

The firelight dancing upon my lids dimmed.

Black Shuck pulled away.

My chest constricted, as if cinched by an over-laced corset, and my teeth sank into my lower lip. The dogs' claws clicked across the floor, away from my side, and I wanted to cry out for them to remain with me, but words abandoned me, so I sprang upright, desperate and fearful.

They had seated themselves before the far corner of the room, their tails sliding back and forth across the floor with unperturbed delight, the way they might when greeting a welcomed guest.

Before them, shrouded and featureless in shadow, a figure stood against the wall.

Neither myself nor the other moved, but I knew it to be regarding me with the same intensity I was watching it. As my sight adjusted to the darkened room, details became more prominent, its petiteness, the long hair, an outline of a dress, and the initial shock waned into an apprehensive curiosity reinforced by my pair's receptiveness.

"Morwen?" Her name came from me as a whisper.

Her movement was stilted and slow, but she nodded once.

My throat bobbed painfully. "You were the one singing earlier, weren't you? You wished me to find those letters."

Again, she made the laboured motion and my dogs whimpered impatiently, bowing their heads in an invitation to be pet, but she made no move to comply.

"Why? What can I do?"

She tried to answer then, but spoke in a low rasp that scratched its way from her neck, a startling and ill fit for the young girl pictured on her poster. Whatever her reply, I did not understand it, and shook my head helplessly. Her form twitched, agitated at my incomprehension, and she repeated herself with great strain.

"Bell."

"Bell?" I ran the word over my tongue, but it might as well have been a foreign one.

"Bell!" she said again, mustering what urgency she could in that ruined voice.

"Is there one in High Hearth?" I asked, but was met with only more stiff twitching. I stepped forward, hands held out entreatingly. "On the grounds? Where is it? What am I to do with it?"

My onslaught of questions ended in a grating gasp from Morwen and she dropped into a crouch, head buried protectively between her arms.

"Forgive me," I pleaded, lowering myself as well, "I did not mean to--"

The speed with which my pair spun around, lips curled, startled me. I toppled, landing hard on my backside, and then, not for an instant fearing I was the object of their ire, turned toward the door where their wrath was aimed.

Through the small opening I'd left, a sliver of pale face, twisted into silent fury, scowled from the dark hallway.

Cold emanated from that hateful visage, so heavy I feared it would smother the fire and plunge us into pitch black. The dogs continued to sound their deep warning and I looked to Morwen again, seeking both to console the girl and beg for further explanation, but she was gone, and when I turned back to the door, it too stood empty.

Despite the fire's resurgence, the cold lingered long after.

***

We remained in the parlour for the rest of the night. I kept the fire burning until dawn. What little sleep I found, huddled in that armchair, was broken by overattentiveness toward the house's every sound. Whenever I woke, new beads of sweat dotting my brow and heart leaping, it was to find my pair lying, shield-like, between myself and the door.

I watched the first light of day rise through the tall windows, but there was little rejoicing to be had in its arrival. Day or night, it did not matter.

The curse of High Hearth did not sleep.

Nor do I because of it, I thought bitterly.

My head throbbed with want of rest, my stomach for food, and it was with the greatest reluctance I roused myself toward the kitchen, where I fried fat slabs of bacon and toasted bread in their grease. It was the accompanying coffee, however, that I truly craved, and greedily drank a cup before my breakfast had finished cooking. Once the ache behind my eyes had lessened, I prepared a second cupful of coffee, plated my meal, and abandoned all shows of decorum by returning with them to the parlour to eat.

I could only hope the act would not summon forth Mother herself to join the spirits of the house in haunting me with her disappointment.

***

Save for the briefest trek outdoors for the sake of my pair, I did not stray from the parlour for many an hour. It was with quiet contemplation that I sat, hardly moving, as if my stillness might inspire the same of the house. My thoughts were a maze of dead ends, blank corridors, stone walls, trapping me within myself until I felt impotent with all that I did not know.

High Hearth was a horrible puzzle, made of uneven edges that fought against its piecing together, leaving me always with more questions when a new part revealed itself.

"Bell," I repeated yet again, making no more sense of it than I had the previous hundred times I'd said it aloud.

The thought of going on another hunt through my great-aunt's things repelled me at my every sense. The prospect alone was demoralizing in its magnitude, but I was also held captive by a new conviction, the roots of which had taken hold in the night and continued to deepen.

I had awakened something in this house, and the more I sought to understand it, the more it resisted, resented, and, in its anger, it took power.

As was so often the case, it was the hounds that pulled me outward again.

Black Shuck stood in one of the front facing windows and, when he expelled a soft, guarded bark, Cerberus joined him. Their snorting and huffing drew me to their side to see a cart coming slowly up the drive. The driver had adorned an Inverness cape to keep out the worst of the damp, dreary afternoon, but the tall hat and full moustache were at once familiar, and I hurried outside to meet him, the dogs at my heels.

"Mr. Bentley!"

The exuberance with which I greeted him caught him unprepared and he reined the horse to a sharp stop. After a wary look toward the hounds, he climbed down from the cart's bench. "Good Heavens, Mrs. Fellowes! Are you alright?"

"I fear that I'm not."

"Forgive my saying so, but you look as if you've not slept since last we met."

I had not stopped to consider my appearance, left untended for almost two days, and made a perfunctory show of smoothing my blouse. "You shan't believe what I'm about to tell you, Mr. Bentley, but I implore you to listen in full before passing judgement."

"Has it to do with Mr. Kenzie?" he asked, and the swift directness with which he spoke made my stomach turn.

"Mr. Kenzie?"

"The parish vicar. He'd made it known that he was coming here, but I overheard his cook in the shop this morning stating his horse returned, but she's seen no sign of the man himself. She was considering going to the police. I decided to come first to speak with you. Tell me true, Mrs. Fellowes, and I will help you as I can: did something occur between yourself and Mr. Kenzie?"

"No," I said, aghast even at his suggestion. "He did visit, but only for a short time, until--" I faltered, keenly aware of how absurd my next statement would sound to a man so learned as a solicitor, whose very business dealt solely in measurable fact, but he nodded, encouraging me on. I took a breath to temper my mind and speech.

"I don't know what happened to the vicar upon his departure, but while here, he was accosted by--"

Mr. Bentley's bespectacled eyes moved immediately to the dogs and I laid a defensive hand on each of their shoulders.

"--my great-aunt."

The good solicitor opened his mouth, considered me from beneath furrowed brow, then closed it again. He tilted his head toward the ground, hiding beneath the brim of his hat, and with a most gentle tone, said, "Have you been unwell, Mrs. Fellowes?"

The noise I made then was one of such pure vexation I doubted I'd ever be able to repeat it again by choice. Upon sensing my displeasure, my pair stiffened, their weight shifting between their paws. Mr. Bentley swept his hat from his head and went practically prostrate in his apology, but I waved it away.

"I am aware how it sounds, but were you to spend any amount of time here, you would know what I say is true. High

Hearth is haunted. I did not want to believe it myself, but I have seen and heard things, Mr. Bentley, and I believe it stems from Emmeline."

"I'm sure you've had some experiences that might seem odd to someone unaccustomed to the country life," he offered meekly. "Manors such as this one have a way of trapping sounds…"

He trailed off, wilting beneath the glower I'd settled on him.

"I am not some chattering ninny bird prone to flights of fancy, Mr. Bentley. I am perfectly capable of determining what is merely the wind and what is something more. How glad I would be were it all only my imagination, but that is not the case. If you are unwilling to hear me out, then I bid you good day."

He took my reprimand with head bent and hat clutched tight at his chest. Had I not been so incensed, I might have experienced some measure of guilt at cowing the man thusly, but I lacked the energy and patience. Perhaps he would think me mad, *hysterical*, but I would not go unheard for the sake of perception.

"You are unconventional, Mrs. Fellowes," he said at last, "but I do not believe you would be so passionate about such a matter without true and serious provocation. I am sorry."

Taken aback by his contriteness, I inclined my head slightly in acknowledgment.

"Tell me, then, what has transpired since I left, so I can better understand your situation."

"Thank you," I said, and there was much relief at the anticipation of being heard. "But first, I must ask you something. You were my great-aunt's solicitor for a number of years, correct?"

"That's right."

I stepped forward and he straightened, unsettled by my scandalous proximity. "Does the word 'bell' hold any significance for you?"

Chapter Eleven

There was, as it turned out, no bell upon High Hearth's property, and there hadn't been since the dismissal of the housekeeper and her son.

"Mrs. Bell had been employed here for much of her life, her son for the entirety of his," Mr. Bentley said.

"And now? Where are they?"

He stroked one corner of his moustache in thought. "They moved to a cottage in the village. But what have they to do with anything?"

"I must speak with them. Today, now. Can you take me?"

"It would be an hour and some to make the journey."

"You must make it anyway, allow me to accompany you. I need to speak with Mrs. Bell. I will explain along the way."

I made as if to pass him and Mr. Bentley cleared his throat, stopping me with an apologetically upheld finger. "I mean no offense…"

"I don't have the time to take any, so please just speak your mind."

"Normally I would not comment on such a thing, but...I cannot in good conscience bring you in such a state."

"And what state would that be, Mr. Bentley?" I whirled on him, antagonized. "Afraid? Exhausted? Stretched thin and brittle as parchment?"

"Your dress," he said, at last speaking with the frankness I desired of him.

It only served to stoke my frustration. "Were I a man--"

"But you are not, Mrs. Fellowes," Mr. Bentley interrupted, and despite his uncomfortable fidgeting, I finally caught a glimpse of the stalwart solicitor behind the quill man's spectacles. Taking advantage of my silence, he more gently continued, "Regardless, were you a man, I would say the same. Granted, it would not be quite so significant an observation, I agree. However, there is already some distrust associated with you, and should you appear before the townspeople like so, your credibility will be all but gone. I do not speak so to judge, but to advise: do not give them more reason to turn against you. Your great-aunt has already sullied the waters enough as it is."

I let my arms hang limp at my sides and looked down at myself, at the wrinkles, stains, and smudges that had come to mar my clothing. I imagined my person fared little better. Necessarily chastened, I splayed my fingers across my forehead and pressed my thumb to my temple.

"I am sorry, Mr. Bentley. I have been far too harsh in the face of your unfailing kindness. I only wish I did not have to cater to such superficial concerns whilst I am so preoccupied. If you would wait for me here, I will hurry inside and change."

"Of course," he agreed, moustache drooping with visible relief at my defusing.

At the entrance to the house, I paused and turned to him again. "Should you like me to leave one of my hounds with you? As a precaution."

Mr. Bentley cast one look at my pair, who had followed me to stand at the door, and quickly shook his head. "Thank you, but no. I will be quite alright."

"Then I would make a request of you, one you must take seriously."

"Of course."

I drummed my fingers once along the doorframe and grimly met his eyes. "Do not set foot inside this house."

***

Upstairs, I closed myself and my pair in my room and crouched before the trunk containing my clothing. I had not yet attended to their ironing since stuffing them so unceremoniously away and to look at them was to see an ocean of creased and crumpled fabrics. With a sinking heart, I pulled dress after dress from the trunk, but each was in a worse way than the one that had come before. Making my debut in the village in any of them was little better than remaining in my current outfit.

I snapped the trunk shut with a furious sigh and sat upon its top, my chin in my upturned hands.

Although Mr. Bentley did concede in a small way that, had I been of the male sex, the fashion in which I arrived would have not been so important, I doubted he understood the true depth of my complaint. A man arriving in unkempt attire might face some scrutiny, but there would always be a measure of sympathy ascribed to him in attempt to justify it. Perhaps he had no wife to tend his needs, as if his masculinity rendered him incapable of doing so himself, or long working hours had made his appearance an afterthought.

A man has to prove himself deserving of scorn.

A woman has to prove herself above it; and it always begins with her manner of dress.

I could not entirely fault Mr. Bentley's reaction, however. He had seen me first only days before, a being carefully constructed to fit seamlessly into the respectable crowds. How different his welcome might have been had I not taken the time to style myself appropriately. Such thoughts of our meeting, and of what I'd been wearing, sent me hurrying suddenly to the wardrobe, reminded of the only article of clothing that had escaped the trunk.

The brown wool travel gown and its matching jacket, hanging alone like prepared funerial garments, lacked the crispness of a fresh pressed ensemble, but they would serve my purpose well enough.

Before changing, I told the hounds to stay, knowing I would only be a moment, and ran down the hall to the washroom to splash water upon my face. My reflection in the mirror above the basin was that of a colourless woman, careworn, features carved deep with anxious lines. My hair had become a rat's nest knotted atop my head. How different, ghastly, this haunted version of myself looked.

"It's a wonder he recognized me at all," I said, smiling ruefully.

My expression flickered into grit-toothed stiffness as my eyes moved past my reflection, to what lay behind me.

Darkness had grown in one corner of the washroom, like a spread of black mould seeping through the wallpaper, and a biting cold accompanied it. In the curling tendrils fanning outward, the shape of a woman began to take form.

I clutched the sides of the sink, and in the mirror, the shadow slithered from one corner to the other, closer to the door. I dreaded to think what might happen if she reached it before I did, trapping me within that room with her.

Or got out.

"The dogs."

My utterance was little more than a whispered exhale, but it summoned forth a roar. It burned upward, from the depths of my belly, and, even as that thing drew closer, it carried me at a charge through the door.

That swirling shadow could have belonged to Satan himself and still I would not have hesitated to race it down the hall to put myself between it and my pair.

I would not allow her near Cerberus and Black Shuck.

The heavy beat of footsteps followed quickly behind, rattling the floorboards with their violent pursuit. Claws, for there was no other way I would describe them, raked at my hair, catching in its gnarls and tearing, trying to drag me back. A tangled patch was ripped from my scalp and I screamed, both from the searing injury and how near I'd come to falling victim to her wicked grasp.

Her breath was ice upon the back of my neck, a winter wind that meant to envelope and bite and snuff out all warmth.

She hissed when my hounds met me outside my bedroom, their heads cocked, then lowered into snarls that lasted only as long as it took me to force them back and slam the door. I fell to my knees between them, an arm around each of their shoulders, and recited the Lord's prayer with such volume and conviction it would be a wonder Mr. Bentley didn't hear me from outside.

If it did not work to drive her off, I had little, if any, recourse left. What else might I inflict upon a supernatural entity? There seemed to be only one thing at my immediate disposal, uncertain as I was to its effectiveness: should Emmeline come through that door, I would meet her with fists.

It was the most absurd impulse I'd ever had, but one I did not doubt I'd follow through with.

I held the hounds close even after I finished my prayer, studying the doorknob for signs of movement, listening for the creak of a floorboard, but none came. She had made nary a sound since I'd locked myself away, her footsteps gone and her cold faded, and when I felt the dogs relax, so too did I.

"Let us hurry and be out of this house," I muttered to the dogs, my trembling still not entirely quieted, "even if only temporarily."

So as not to keep Mr. Bentley waiting any longer, I dressed and brushed my hair with a grimace. A light touch to the back of my head revealed a tender bare spot, and my fingertips came away with small dots of red. She was growing bolder, more dangerous, but more frightening still than whatever bodily harm she might inflict upon me was the rage.

It coursed from her like water overflowing its well, crashing and surging, and she would see me suffocate in it.

My hands shook as I pinned my hair into a simple twist, arranging it so as to conceal the worst of my encounter. Other than a hat, which served to further hide my wound, I forwent any additional accessories I might have otherwise spent time matching to my gown. At the very least, it was not a look that would attract attention for good or ill, and really, that was all I needed from it. So readied, I and my pair made a hasty exit from High Hearth.

But even after stepping from the confines of the house, I could not rid myself of the sensation we were being watched, and not with a favourable eye. I did not allow myself to turn and search the windows to confirm my suspicions.

The solicitor was already seated upon the cart bench when I made my return. If he *had* heard me, he made no show of it, and I did not immediately mention this latest incident. Doing so while still on the property felt too akin to playing with fire. Like it might feed her.

As I called for the hounds to jump into its back, he sputtered with indignation.

"You mean to bring them?" he asked.

"Of course. They go where I do."

"Perhaps it would be better if they remained," he replied, posture forward leaning to create some distance between himself and Cerberus' curious snout.

I hoisted myself on to the bench beside him. "Mr. Bentley," I said, lemon sweet, "I would sooner leave you here, which is still an option, should you so prefer."

"What will people think, Mrs. Fellowes?" he questioned, a blatant attempt to appeal to my sense of propriety. "They are not exactly a lady's lapdogs."

"Whatever they want, I imagine, perhaps even some of them rightly, but that is a consideration for another time. Now, I implore you: make haste." To better placate the man, I added, "And do not worry yourself over my pair. They will be no trouble, I promise you. I just cannot in good conscience go without them. If something were to happen to them in my absence..."

I could not even give voice to the thought and turned away, knuckles resting heavy against my quivering lips. That I could crack with such little provocation was an embarrassing testament to the weight of my fatigue and the very true nature of my fear.

Perhaps Mr. Bentley was the sort who couldn't abide arguing with an emotional woman. More likely, given what I'd come to understand of him, he was quietly touched by my vulnerability, a rare display not often made public, and he clicked his tongue, sending the cart lurching forward without further comment.

Chapter Twelve

The countryside passed by in silence. Mr. Bentley allowed me my privacy while I once more hardened the tender edges of my mood, made soft by High Hearth's relentlessness. I faced away from him, toward the spanning miles of cliff's edge and the sea beyond, until the cart turned inland and the landscape became a spread of sloping green brightened by a rare break in the heavens.

The sting of my scalp had not yet begun to fade. I was keenly aware of it, this cruel mark of my unwelcome, and it was within that heated pain I began to reforge the iron of my will.

She had attacked me within my own home. Made me unsafe in what should have been my sanctuary against a world that never seemed quite sure what to do with me. She had taken from me one of the rarest and most valuable commodities: my sense of belonging. But worst of all, she had caused great upset to my hounds.

I would never have tolerated such malice from the living; I certainly would not suffer it from the dead.

The wound she had dealt me was a declaration of things to come. If I meant to remain in High Hearth, and I had every intention to, it would not be without a fight. Whatever she wanted, whatever bound her there, I would discover it, then sever her hold on my house.

I gazed then toward the forward horizon with an eagerness that sought to pull it closer by sheer force of will, for the horse's plodding pace was suddenly not near quick enough for my liking.

Sensing my shift in mood, Mr. Bentley tilted his hat so that the brim was no longer between us. Before he could voice any of the questions that played across his rounded features, I spoke.

"I must once again beg your forgiveness. My actions must seem dreadfully strange and I have given little reason for them."

He chose his response with deliberate prudence. "As I stated previously; I do not find you to be a woman of delicate nature. Whatever you have endured must be most dismaying."

"I do not believe in ghosts and the like, Mr. Bentley," I said, staring hard at his profile. "At least, I didn't until coming here. I have not spent a single moment alone in High Hearth since my arrival. I have seen her, Emmeline, and a girl called Morwen, though the latter is benign. Helpful, even, if I understand her intent correctly. There is also my great-uncle."

"He's returned?" Mr. Bentley asked, and I could see the memorized pages of law turning rapidly behind his eyes, trying to determine what that might mean for the estate.

"He's dead," I stated plainly. "And I believe it was my great-aunt's doing."

"That is a bold claim, Mrs. Fellowes, even to make of the deceased."

"And it is not one I would make lightly. The house holds things beyond their spirits. I believe certain memories, ones created during moments of fierce emotion, are etched upon its walls, and if one listens, they will hear High Hearth's bitter secrets. One such instance led me to my great uncle's ghost, left hanging from the cliff side where Emmeline pushed him."

"How could you know it was him? He disappeared decades ago. Perhaps you encountered a vagrant or--"

"Please, Mr. Bentley," I said, but rather than cross, I was merely weary. "Really I would prefer it to have been a vagrant and the rest all products of my city mind unaccustomed to the peculiarities of country life. But I know, to my God fearing soul, what I say is the unfortunate truth. There is darkness in High Hearth, one that has trapped the dead, and it stems from her."

Mr. Bentley stared down at the reins in his hands, his moustache bristling, relaxing, and bristling again as he considered my statement.

"Why?" he asked at last without looking up. "Why would she kill her husband? And who is this 'Morwen' child? I had been Mrs. Parsings' solicitor for nearly twenty years and never heard any such name mentioned."

"That," I replied, "is what I'm hoping Mrs. Bell can tell me."

***

Over the course of our remaining journey, I recounted my harrowing time spent in High Hearth, leading up to the present. Mr. Bentley listened quietly, allowing me to tell my story to completion even as I saw the desire to offer some mundane alternative to my narrative sitting upon the tip of his tongue.

It was only when I unpinned my hat and revealed the bloodied spot hidden beneath my hair that he paled and swallowed any further speculation.

"Why did you not mention that sooner?" he asked. "Should we call upon the doctor?"

"No," I said, affixing my hat back into place. "It is not serious. Now, unless you believe I did this to myself, you will understand why I must speak with Mrs. Bell so urgently."

He agreed with a slap of the reins across the horse's back, hurrying its step.

***

Farmsteads broke up the countryside with low stone walls and wooden fences, behind which sheep and cattle grazed, unconcerned by our passing. The dirt road smoothed beneath us, a telling sign of its more regular use than what surrounded High Hearth. The shingle-roof houses dotting the distance became more frequent, each built closer to the road than the last, until they stood in weathered rows immediately to either side. I commanded the hounds, who had been watching the far off flocks with rapt attention, to lie down, concealing their imposing stature in order to draw less attention.

Homes turned to businesses as we reached the village centre: a haberdashery, millinery, cobbler, the dry goods shop, each fronted by a large window displaying samples of their wares. Much to my impatience, Mr. Bentley pulled the cart to a halt in front of the shop to allow an elderly woman to cross in front of us. When she looked up in thanks, recognition turned her lips upward in a polite smile.

"Afternoon, Crawford," she said with a bob of her head, but her attention on him was short lived. Smile still in place, her gaze moved to me and narrowed just slightly with suspicious curiosity. I recognized that look, the hungry sniffing about for hints of a scandal to later serve as gossip fodder, and her aged status made for a blunt tongue. "And who's this, then? I don't believe I've seen you before."

"No," Mr. Bentley said, sidelong look beseeching me to tolerate the delay. "She's only just arrived. Allow me to introduce Eudora Fellowes, a client of my firm. I'm helping to familiarize her with the village. Mrs. Fellowes, this is Mrs. Agatha Porter."

"A pleasure," I attempted a courteous expression, but felt how thinly it lay upon my features.

"Indeed," Mrs. Porter agreed, her interest having noticeably waned at the mention of our professional relationship. Still, she wasn't quite ready to give up a potential new topic of conversation for her ladies’ circle. "Are you staying in the village, Mrs. Fellowes?"

"No," I replied, hoping with minimum effort my desire to move along wasn't so transparent as to be overtly rude. "I've taken residence at High Hearth."

The frost that came to blanket Mrs. Porter's demeanour was swift, and she tightened her shawl 'round her shoulders. "You're kin to Emmeline Parsings?"

"Distantly so," Mr. Bentley replied quickly, but it did little to thaw Mrs. Porter's newfound perception.

"Well," she said, and paused as if there was more she had wished to say, only to repeat with stiff finality, "Well. I must be going. Do give my regards to your wife, Crawford."

"Of course." He tipped his hat toward her, but she already had her back to us as she crossed toward the baker.

Her hurried departure earned us a few inquisitive looks from those near enough to witness it. Mr. Bentley put them behind us with a click of his tongue, sending the horse into motion again.

"Please don't take it to heart," he said once he was sure we were beyond the woman's hearing. "I tried to warn you of your great-aunt's reputation."

"Were it not my kinship with Emmeline alienating them, it would be some other facet of myself they'd take issue with. Don't worry, Mr. Bentley, I am no stranger to such things."

Under more normal circumstances, I would have preferred to be judged separately from my relation, but I hardly had the mind in that moment to care. After all, what was one more footnote in the curious case of Eudora Fellowes?

***

The Bell cottage was an older but pristinely kept two-story structure of whitewashed stone on the village edge. Tall shrubs and beds of flowers had been lovingly tended into vibrant life, surrounding the house with thick colour and greenery that almost obscured its open front windows, through which drifted the enticing aroma of roasting meat that roused the dogs' interest.

As they reared to stand with front paws on the cart's side, sniffing eagerly, Mr. Bentley implored, "We can leave them here, I trust?"

To this, I nodded, for I had no reason to expect they would not be safe, and commanded them to stay. Their low-wagging tails and soft whines bespoke their unhappiness at my order.

Mr. Bentley halted the cart alongside the fence, completely coated in vines and pink climbing roses, and descended to open the waist-high gate, allowing us entrance on to the property. No sooner had we stepped on to the cobblestone path leading to the front door than it opened, and a man of lean stature with a wind worn complexion came out to meet us.

"You have business here?" he asked, eyeing us dubiously from beneath heavy grey brows.

By his middle-age and the rough nature of his appearance, flecked with dirt and blackened nails, I assumed this was Mrs. Bell's son, who had acted as groundskeeper at High Hearth. Mr. Bentley confirmed it so with his greeting.

"Thomas," he said, removing his hat. "I'm not sure you remember me, as we only met once. I'm Crawford Bentley, I was--"

"The missus' solicitor," Thomas finished for him, although the remembrance did not warm him to us. "I recognize you now. Gave me and Mum our papers and told us to be on our way just about the day after Lady Parsings hopped the twig."

"An unfortunate duty that gave me no pleasure," Mr. Bentley replied evenly.

Thomas spat out of the side of his mouth, content to allow that to serve as his answer.

Mr. Bentley cleared his throat and made a small gesture toward the door. "Is your mother in? We'd like a word."

"Who's we?"

"I'm Eudora Fellowes," I cut in to introduce myself, and Thomas settled into a humourless smirk at my forthrightness. "I inherited High Hearth and would like to speak with your mother regarding its...history."

It seemed wise to avoid the subject of ghosts until I'd had a chance to gauge the quality of Mrs. Bell's person and her receptiveness. I did not want to be driven off as a mad woman before I'd even gotten to speak with her.

He ran his tongue noisily over his teeth and shrugged. "Don't think she'll have much to say, really. It's your problem now, isn't it?"

"Please." I clasped my hands contritely at my breast. "Ask her if she will see us, I beg you."

"Now that's a treat; the lady of the manor begging me. Wait 'til I tell the lads at the pub."

"Sir--"

"*Sir*, is it? Well, I'll tell you what, Bentley, wherever you got her from is an improvement over the Lady Parsings. Got a real polite streak for the small folk, this one."

His cavalier repartee had quickly become tiresome and before Mr. Bentley could attempt gentler placations, I heatedly said, "I have come to speak with your mother. Either you will cease this childish nonsense and let her know of our visit, or I shall start calling for her myself, and I shan't be peaceful about it."

"Mrs. Fellowes," Mr. Bentley muttered in disproval.

Thomas folded his arms across his chest and leaned against the wall, as if inviting me to have my tantrum. "What's so important?"

"I would like to find out what she knows about Morwen."

His cocksure posture tightened at the girl's name. "Morwen?" He licked his lips. "What...why…" He stammered, then gathered his thoughts beneath a bewildered scowl. "How do you know that name?"

"I'll be happy to explain," I said, secretly pleased at having unseated him so, "if I can speak with your mother."

Hard indecision stiffened his shoulders and clenched his calloused hands into loose fists, until, with another spat, he pushed the door behind him open and motioned for us to follow.

Chapter Thirteen

Natural light filled the ground floor, a single room that served as kitchen, dining room, and parlour. Combined with the savoury scent of the roast and the cosy assortment of furniture arranged throughout the space, it was idyllic in its rustic simplicity. The elderly woman standing by the stove, aproned, a wooden spoon in hand, with her snow-white hair piled neatly into a bun at the back of her head, only added to the image of quaint, pastoral haven.

"Mum," Thomas raised his voice, drawing the woman's attention from her cooking. "Some guests to see you." To Mr. Bentley and myself, he brusquely explained, "Her hearing's not so good. You have to speak up for her to hear you proper."

Concern fluttered across her face, although it did not diminish the more permanent glow of grandmotherly hospitality she immediately radiated. "Were we expecting anyone?"

"No," Mr. Bentley answered for us, "and we do apologize for any imposition we might be causing."

"Oh, nonsense." Mrs. Bell brightened. "The more the merrier, as they say."

"The fewer, the better fare," Thomas spoke the proverb to its completion, at which Mrs. Bell clucked her tongue with a warning wave of her spoon.

"Blessed are we who are able to share our bounties, Thomas," she said with affectionate patience before once more addressing us. "I've prepared mutton, carrots, and potatoes for dinner. A bit early, I'll grant, but why should that stop us, hmm? It'll be ready shortly. As you're already here, I expect you'll be joining us."

"That's really not necessary, Mrs. Bell," I said, pricked with guilt we had arrived with such inconvenient timing. "I only wish to ask you some questions."

She was already rustling about in the cupboards. "That'll be the conversation sorted, then, Mrs…" A short-lived frown deepened the wrinkles around her mouth. "I'm sorry, dear. Who are you?"

"I'm Eudora Fellowes; Emmeline Parsings was my great-aunt. This is Mr. Bentley--"

"Oh, of course," she tutted ruefully. "Mr. Bentley, how could I have forgotten? You were so kind upon my lady's passing. It's a pleasure to see you again." It was with such genuine joy shining in her eyes that she looked upon me next. "And you, Mrs. Fellowes! What a delight. I doubt you remember, but we did meet once, long ago. You were only a small girl then."

"I'm sorry; I recall very little from then."

"Not a surprise." Mrs. Bell nodded, her airs more sombre. "It was only a short visit as Lady Parsings wasn't in the most welcoming of moods."

"Nothing out of the ordinary there," Thomas said.

"Mind your tongue, son. She always did right by us."

Thomas looked ready to spit again, but instead excused himself to wash for dinner. He ascended the cottage's narrow staircase with a lingering glance over his shoulder.

"Don't pay any mind to Thomas. He and the lady, God rest her soul, were often at odds. I think he reminded her too much of her own little one." She wiped her hands on her apron and sighed. "Forgive me, I can talk enough for all of us if you let me. You said you had questions?"

"Yes, about High Hearth and my great-aunt."

Mrs. Bell tugged out one of the two chairs set around the dining table and motioned for me to sit. At the first sign of my declination, she rounded to me, took me firmly by the crook of my arm, and guided me to it. The endearing earnest of her character made it impossible to rebuke such unwarranted familiarity and I did as she desired, although it was not without some awkwardness. I again cursed my timing as I was made to claim one of the Bells' places at their own table.

"You're living there, then? High Hearth?" Mrs. Bell queried while plating modest portions of the meal.

"I am. Mr. Bentley told me you were employed there for many years."

"Oh, yes," she said, smile soft with nostalgia. "The lady took me in when I was eighteen. I was in the family way, you see, but unwed - no need to blush so, Mr. Bentley, I hold no shame over the act that gave me my Thomas - and going door to door begging for work. The housekeeper tried to turn me away like all the rest, but Lady Parsings put a stop to that. She was the only mistress who'd see me. She hired me that same day and I didn't leave again until after the good Lord had called her to His side."

"So you knew Emmeline well."

Mrs. Bell whisked the plates to the table with practiced ease, despite age bending and swelling the knuckles of her fingers. "After fifty years, I'd say so. I started as a scullery maid, but the lady and I, we understood each other better than most. She made me her lady's maid after Thomas was born."

"Understood each other?"

My prodding, lightly done as it was, had struck a nerve with the elderly woman and she dragged her hands in brisk strokes down her apron. "Your aunt wasn't the most traditional sort. Nothing wrong with her, mind you," she said, as if I meant to challenge her. "She just had her own way of thinking. I suppose I did, too. Unusual as it might sound to someone of your station, Mrs. Fellowes, we could talk to one another as though we were no different than a pair of sisters instead of lady and help."

She could not have said anything more pleasing to my ears. That she'd held such a bond with Emmeline brought me great hope, but also gave me pause. No one else I had ever spoken to regarding my great-aunt recalled her with such fondness, not even my father, with whom she'd shared blood. It was difficult to reconcile this version of Emmeline from the one I had come to know.

Thomas' skulking return interrupted our conversation as his mother informed him Mr. Bentley and myself were to take dinner at the table and Thomas and herself would eat in the nearby armchairs with the centre table between them. Upon being made aware of the arrangement, Thomas' scowl deepened but, perhaps for the sake of his mother, he held his tongue.

I had eaten many a fine meal in my time, some prepared by the most sought-after chefs in the country, but few came close to the satisfaction derived from Mrs. Bell's cooking. What she lacked in finesse, missing the herb sprouts and spices afforded to those in better stocked kitchens, she made up for with sheer heartiness. The mutton, thickly cut and covered generously in rich gravy, was tender, and the vegetables made flavourful from the meat's drippings.

I ate in small bites, the further subject of my great-aunt trapped behind uncertain lips. Bringing such unpleasant topics as the ones I carried from High Hearth up over dinner hardly seemed appropriate and I had not the faintest idea of how to raise them to this sweet woman. A look across to Mr. Bentley, who stroked habitually at his moustache despite its cleanliness, revealed him to be as unsure as I.

Thomas saved us from additional strife by cutting directly to the heart of the matter. Around a partially chewed mouthful, he loudly asked, "Have you told them about Morwen yet?"

Mrs. Bell's knife scratched across her plate. She looked up sharply, her complexion dulling to a waxy pale. "What?"

"That's what's brought them here," he said. "They want to know about the girl."

"Nothing to tell, really." Mrs. Bell's answer, higher in octave than previous statements, was clipped. She maintained a pointed gaze upon her food, but did not resume eating. "She stayed at High Hearth for a time. That is all."

Gently, I laid aside my cutlery and turned fully toward Mrs. Bell, who steadfastly refused to meet my imploring eyes. "I have not been forthright with you, Mrs. Bell, and for that I do apologize. My great-aunt did bring me here, but I fear it is not due to any passive desire to reminisce about the woman. I come because something terrible has laid claim to High Hearth and I believe you are key to helping me undo it."

"I don't know what you're talking about," she said stiffly.

"I have reason to think you do," I replied, soft in tone and posture to avoid the appearance of accusation. "*Morwen* thinks you do."

The elderly woman's lip quivered at the mention of that name. She snatched a handkerchief from the pocket of her apron and dabbed it firmly over her mouth.

Seeing her so distressed did equally distress me, for she had been so kind as to open her home before even knowing my identity, but I could not relent.

"She -- they remain, Mrs. Bell," I pushed with as much urgency as I dared. "I need to know why."

Thomas had also set his utensils down and leaned forward in his chair, observing with keen intent, but not stopping my line of questioning. I could see in the tense curl of his fingers, however, that I tread a fine line. Rough as his edges might've been, there was no doubting his dedication to his mother, or that he would not hesitate to remove me from their home if I proved too much of a nuisance.

"You've already made your mind up about her. I see it in your face," she said, voice trembling.

"No, I--"

"Lady Parsings was a good woman," she insisted. "After all she had been through, she was still a good woman."

"What had she been through? Please, help me understand."

With her passions stoked, Mrs. Bell pushed away from her chair and paced to the stove, apron wrung in gnarled hands. She picked up the pan the vegetables had cooked in, set it down, only to pluck up the serving spoon and replace it as well, as if she were searching for some task with which to distract herself, but was unable to focus enough to follow through. Mr. Bentley started to rise with the apologetic meekness of one meaning to remove himself from an uncomfortable situation, but I angled my head in a subtle shake, urging him to remain both in place and quiet. His moustache, purveyor of all emotion, curved downward, but he sank back into his seat.

"Mrs. Bell--"

"She never wanted to marry." She spoke with her back to us, hands gripping the countertop's edge so tight they'd gone white. "Nor have children. It was no secret to her family, and how they shamed her for it. The things they said to her, called her. They went so far as to call upon their vicar to drive the devil's influence out of her. It was only by luck they wed her to as good a man as Lord Parsings, but he wanted his heir, and he…" Mrs. Bell covered her face with both hands, overcome for a moment by her memories.

I thought Thomas might go to comfort her, but he remained unmoved, jaw set in a grim line. There was something expectant in the way he watched her, the kind of rigidness that comes from waiting for a truth left long unspoken.

Mrs. Bell lowered her hands, and when she spoke next, her affect was flat and cool. "I only came into their employ three years after Master Thaddeus was born, but there was never any doubt that she loved that boy with all she had. He was her world. One she'd never wanted, true enough, but that she grew to love with such ferocity it frightened her at times. And then...he caught the fever. He was only ten."

She turned to face us, pain pooling as tears in the deep valleys of her face. "Imagine: forced to bring a child into this world, made to love it until your heart has no room for any others, then he is snatched away by God's own hand. She was lost, her will to live buried alongside her son. There was no joy left for her. Only that house, where she was made to walk its every room with his memory, and her husband. Do you know what grows in the hollow place left by love, Mrs. Fellowes?"

"Desperation," I replied, so soft I doubt she heard me.

I had been there too, that desolate place that follows death. After my mother's passing, I had been like a ghost myself, unsure I would ever know happiness again, and I was frantic for something to give me purpose. Little by little, I had found myself again, through my books, my art, my hounds. It was them, Cerberus and Black Shuck, who had pulled me most completely from the dark.

But a child is meant to outlive her parents.

"That is why she called upon Morwen," I said, louder this time to ensure it reached Mrs. Bell.

In doing so, I was reminded of the fight between lord and lady that had embedded itself into the fabric of High Hearth. My great-uncle had denied Emmeline's request to summon the medium, thus cutting off what she perceived to be her only connection to their late son. Without his approval, she could never have brought Morwen, and Thaddeus through her, home.

I did not make mention of Lord Parsings' fate, fearing Mrs. Bell would take offense at the implication her lady was the murderess of her own husband.

Her nod was a singular, reluctant motion. "The letters started coming some months following his death. The promises they made...I knew them to be ungodly, and the lady did, too. She ignored those first ones, but they became more personal, telling her things only the young master would've been able to share."

"Like 'Jenny'," I said, and then, upon her questioning glance, added, "I found -- or rather, I was shown to the letters. She had kept them."

"Jenny was the housecat. Master Thaddeus loved her very much."

"Why'd the lady drown it after he died then?" Thomas asked sourly.

I scowled, irritated that he would interrupt in such a way that might derail the conversation, and interjected quickly, "So Morwen must truly have been a medium to reveal such an intimate detail."

Mrs. Bell drifted back to her armchair, and in the shadows cast by the fading sun, she seemed an older woman than the one who'd met us. "No," she said from behind her fingers, spread wearily across her mouth. "It was an evil trick of greed upon grief and nothing more."

"But how? If she and her guardian knew these things-"

"The scullery maid," Thomas replied in his mother's stead. "She'd heard tell of a Welshman and his ward going about, making such grand claims, and she wrote to him in secret. Told him all he needed to know to get him and that girl into the house in return for a share of what he made. Once they had her good and convinced, Lady Parsings paid a pretty penny to keep Morwen for her own."

"How did you come to know this?" I asked, looking between mother and son.

"The girl herself. The little grifter had some soul in her after all."

"She was only a child, Thomas," Mrs. Bell reprimanded him sharply. "She was as much a victim as my lady."

"What then? What became of her?"

Thomas looked ready to answer, but Mrs. Bell proved quicker, and the more she spoke, the more defensive she became, as if with her words she was erecting a wall between us. "My lady loved that little girl. She clothed her in silks and satins, fed her only the best, bought her more than she could ever want. They went everywhere together. She was afraid of the dark, Morwen was, so Lady Parsings let her hold on to her gown as they went up the steps every night so she could keep her eyes closed. She let her share her bed. She even had Morwen teach her a lullaby in Welsh so she could sing her to sleep. She was more a mother to Morwen than the woman who birthed her."

"I understand, but--"

"That's all you need to know about my lady," Mrs. Bell said definitively. "I do believe it's time we said goodnight."

"Mrs. Bell--"

"Goodnight, Mrs. Fellowes. I do hope you find peace in High Hearth."

"Please--"

Once more, she took hold of the crook of my arm, but this time there was nothing gentle in her guidance as she pulled me to my feet. Mr. Bentley, unaided, followed suit, and while I still attempted to protest, Mrs. Bell thrust us from her home.

Chapter Fourteen

Were it not for Mr. Bentley, having been shuffled out behind me, standing between myself and the door, I might have turned and started banging my fist against it. So blocked, however, I could only call past the solicitor, entreating Mrs. Bell to reconsider.

Mr. Bentley winced and cupped his ear nearest to me. "Please, Mrs. Fellowes, let us not make a spectacle of ourselves."

"But there is so much more I must know," I said, furious and embarrassed in equal measure at the tears blurring my vision. "We cannot just leave!"

"And yet we must," he replied with hushed firmness. "Mrs. Bell has made it clear we are no longer welcome. For the moment, anyway. Allow her, and yourself, the opportunity to calm and reflect. Cooler heads will prevail."

The prospect of having met another impasse weighed like stones in my heart, pulling it toward the pit of my stomach, and I stifled a disheartened sob into the back of my wrist.

"Come, Mrs. Fellowes." Mr. Bentley, discomfited as he was by my outburst, offered his arm. "It will be dark soon. Instead of returning to High Hearth tonight, allow me to book you a room at the hotel. You and your dogs can get some proper rest and, perhaps, we can come back in the morning and see if Mrs. Bell isn't feeling more agreeable."

Reluctantly I linked my arm through his, letting that convey my acquiescence, and we walked the path back to the road.

***

The hounds crowded at the end of the cart, excited by our approach, and I withdrew from Mr. Bentley to greet them with equal, albeit more subdued, affection. I rested my forehead first against Black Shuck's, until Cerberus pushed him aside and took his place. Unsurprisingly, the good solicitor bypassed them entirely and waited for me by the driver's bench.

With the breath of despair so hot upon my neck, I closed my eyes, seeking momentary solace in my pair's nearness.

Suddenly alert, Cerberus took his head from mine and looked over my shoulder. Instead of trying to reclaim my attention while his brother was otherwise preoccupied, Black Shuck did the same. Neither made a sound, and it was under the scrutiny of my canine sentries that Thomas appeared at the roadside.

Concerned he'd come to tell us off for loitering, Mr. Bentley attempted to intervene. "We were about to leave--"

But Thomas cut in. "Only reason I let you talk to Mum is because I hoped she'd finally tell it true."

"Tell what true?" I asked, betraying my eagerness with a step toward him. The dogs huffed softly, but a waved hand sent them to their haunches.

"What happened to Morwen and the others."

"Others?" Mr. Bentley and I traded a quizzical glance.

"Lord Parsings, the scullery maid. The other mediums." Thomas cast a furtive look toward the cottage. "After Morwen, the lady brought in two more in the years that followed, an Irish woman and some southern toff who thought quite highly of herself. They all disappeared. Mum said they'd left, but I never believed it."

My pulse had come alive in my veins. "Why not?"

"Their things were still there. I saw them, hidden away in unused rooms."

"What do you thi--"

He did not let me finish my question. "You know the study door downstairs? The one that's always locked?"

"Yes?"

"The lady used to spend hours alone in that room. I was never allowed in, never told what was in it, but I'd hear her talking and talking, even though she was supposed to be alone. When we were leaving High Hearth after she died, I saw Mum sneak this from her ring." He took hold of my wrist and pressed a cold key into my palm. "Mum doesn't know I knew about this, or where it was. I wasn't sure she would -- could -- tell you, so I...take it. Open it. Whatever Lady Parsings was hiding, it's in that room."

I closed my fingers tight around the key and clutched it to my chest as if it were treasure. "Thank you."

"Whatever you find," he said, throat bobbing, "don't bring it back here. Once you leave, you're gone. You won't trouble Mum over it anymore. She won't say what happened there, not even to me, but I know it's sat heavy enough on her already."

"Why would you do this?" Mr. Bentley could not withhold his curiosity.

Thomas rubbed the back of his neck. "I liked Morwen. She...she was always kind to me, even though she didn't have to be. Even stopped the lady from hitting me a time or two. I always wondered what happened to her, but Mum just repeated the lady and said she ran away. If what you're saying is true, she deserves better than to be stuck there, with her." His confession made, he became gruff once more. "None of this comes back to Mum. Now go."

Before he could change his mind, I clambered on to the cart bench and urged Mr. Bentley to do the same. As we prepared to leave, Thomas stopped us one last time.

"Those your dogs, Mrs. Fellowes?"

"They are."

"Good. Keep them close," he said, his humours black. "Lady Parsings was terrified of dogs."

***

The generously titled "hotel" was a tall and narrow building near the village centre, the ground floor of which also served as the pub. The white painted exterior had greyed beneath an unwashed veneer and the windows were in sore need of a thorough scrubbing. The front door had been left propped open to take advantage of the balmy evening and from within came the steady murmur of voices and clinking dinnerware.

In my past, I might have balked at the prospect of staying in such a location, lacking, as it seemed to be, in all but the most basic necessities, but potential unlaundered linens and pest bites would be a small price to pay for a night away from High Hearth.

Misery makes beggars of us all.

"If you'll wait here with your dogs, I'll procure you a room," Mr. Bentley said.

"This is very kind of you," I replied. "All of it, and I cannot think how I shall ever properly repay you."

Behind his moustache, Mr. Bentley turned a bashful shade of pink, and excused himself with a bumbling, "Think nothing of it."

As I watched him disappear inside the hotel, it struck me as criminal that a man so genuinely good as Crawford Bentley was such a stranger to gratitude.

While I awaited his return, I turned the key over in my hand, as if I meant to memorize its shape and pattern by touch alone. Thomas had said they'd been dismissed, perhaps unexpectedly so, within days of Emmeline's death. Being made to leave the property with such immediacy would not have given Mrs. Bell time to empty the study. Her only other option, then, would have been to keep people out for as long as possible.

But why? What could she be hiding on her lady's behalf?

She had to have known it would only be a short-term solution. Or had she hoped High Hearth would remain empty? That I, or another like me, would never be found and, thus, never open the door, forever maintaining Emmeline's secrets.

A raised voice drew my attention from the key towards the pub. I was ready to dismiss it as an overindulgent patron when Mr. Bentley was escorted roughly to the door by a man almost as broad as he was tall.

"This is ridiculous," Mr. Bentley, as riled as I had ever seen him, proclaimed. My pair, drawn by his upset, began to stir, but I was quick to snap them to attention, fearing any involvement from them would only provoke matters further.

The man sent Mr. Bentley stumbling over the threshold with an effortless nudge. "Told you, we ain't got no rooms." His eyes, made small by the overlap of his brow, slid to me. "Not for no Parsings."

"I have told you; she is *not* a Parsings. She hardly knew the woman at all!"

Unswayed by Mr. Bentley's argument, the barman kicked aside the stool holding open the door and let it fall closed between them.

Mr. Bentley, ruddy with aggravation, threw his hands up with a wordless shout, then, made self-conscious by his loss of composure, straightened his spine and his hat, and marched back to the cart.

"Scoundrels and fools," he said with vicious scorn. "The lot of them."

"Don't trouble yourself. I am hardly offended by what they think." I attempted to soothe his temper, but his mood continued to worsen as we pulled away.

"It is not offense I am worried about. It's…" He trailed off, teeth clenched.

"It's what?"

"I will only ask this once more, Mrs. Fellowes, and I trust you will answer with complete sincerity: Did something happen between yourself and Mr. Kenzie?"

"No," I said vehemently. "It's as I said before: he left following an encounter with Emmeline."

He sighed, rclaxing into a slump. "I believe you," he said. "But his housekeeper has been going about suggesting otherwise, and Mrs. Porter has made it known she met you today and claims she felt your great aunt's presence in you. It has left a most...unkind impression."

"And the rest believe such madness?"

"Small minds are easily swayed. Until Mr. Kenzie returns, there is little we can do to convince them otherwise."

"And if he does not return, Mr. Bentley, what then?"

He frowned down at the reins. "You doubt he will?"

"I do not know what to think," I admitted, and in doing so, came to a hard revelation. Staying in the village, where already I had been tainted by my blood, would not serve any purpose. Mrs. Bell would tell me no more.

Thomas had already given me everything I needed.

Taking notice of my expression, dour as it was, Mr. Bentley began to state we would make other nightly accommodations for me, but already I knew it was a wasted effort.

There was only one place left for me if I wanted to learn what happened to Mr. Kenzie, Morwen, and the others.

Only one woman who truly had the answers I sought.

"That won't be necessary," I said.

"Where will you go, then?"

I looked to the dark horizon. "Home."

"You mean High Hearth?" he asked, aghast. "No. No, I cannot allow it. It's already nightfall, the road will be dangerous. Please, reconsider. I have a guest room in my home, I can have my wife--"

"You are my solicitor, Mr. Bentley, and even, if I may be so bold, my friend, but you are not my father. And even if you were, long gone are the days that I need to be *allowed* to do anything. Besides," I turned on the bench to pet Black Shuck and Cerberus once each before continuing, "I will not be going alone."

"At least let me take you," he said.

"No," I replied. "I thank you for the offer, but I cannot put you in such danger."

"Mrs. Fellowes--"

"This is not a debate, Mr. Bentley. I am merely informing you of what's going to happen."

"There must be something I can do."

"There is, actually." I faced him with a slight smile. "Do you remember when I asked you for a bicycle?"

Chapter Fifteen

Mr. Bentley proved persistent in his entreaties to accompany me back to High Hearth, but I held firm, refusing to even entertain the idea. It was only once I dismounted from the cart with my hounds and began to stride resolutely homeward that he relented, finally accepting my decision as indisputable.

The promised bicycle was at his home, a terraced house packed snuggly down a side lane off the village centre. It had been a gift for his wife, he explained as we traversed the darkened street, but she had taken little interest in it, trusting more in her feet than a pair of narrow wheels.

"You are sure she won't mind my taking it?" I asked, once more anxious over transgressing social boundaries.

"Not at all," he said. "In fact, she would thank you for doing so. It's a fine machine, but makes for poor furniture. We'll both be glad to see our entryway free of it."

The exterior of the Bentley residence, reflective of the man himself, was understated and simple, perfectly in line with those on either side of it. Light shone in a downstairs window from behind lace curtains. At the approaching creak of the cart, the curtains twitched briefly, then the front door opened. A short, plump woman, Mrs. Bentley by my assumption, stepped out, her round face creased from long hours of concern.

"Crawford," she exclaimed, her relief palpable. "Thank the Lord! When you didn't come home for supper, I--" When she saw that he was not alone on the cart bench, her cheeks flushed with embarrassment and she hid them behind her hands. "Oh, dear. I wasn't aware you'd be bringing a guest. I've already done the washing. But I could put the kettle on? Oh, dear…"

"It's alright, Tillie, she's not going to be staying long," Mr. Bentley said as we climbed down from the cart. "This is Eudora Fellowes. Mrs. Fellowes, my wife, Tillie."

"Oh, Mrs. Fellowes." Her face somehow found a new shade of red to turn, and she touched her uncurled hair and brushed fretfully at her skirts. "Yes, of course, Crawford has told me so much about you. I'm sorry for my appearance. Had I known you were coming, I would have made myself more presentable. Oh, please don't think poorly of me or Crawford. I--"

Mr. Bentley laid a hand on his wife's forearm and squeezed gently, his expression one of exasperated affection. She returned it with a bashful smile, her flutters calming now that he was at her side.

It was obvious in that single shared look, oblivious to all but each other, that I was witnessing two halves of a whole: the steady, reliant quill man and his doting, excitable wife.

And I knew beyond doubt I had made the correct choice in denying Mr. Bentley's company to the dangers of High Hearth.

Mr. Bentley made as if to step inside. "If it's alright with you, Mrs. Fellowes is going to take your bicycle."

"*Only* if it's alright with you," I added pointedly.

"Thank Heavens!" Mrs. Bentley said. "If you can make use of it, please do." To Mr. Bentley, she dipped her head apologetically and tempered her enthusiasm. "I'm sorry, dear. I know you meant well, and I do appreciate it, but I think we both know I'll never be the bicycling sort."

While the solicitor went to retrieve the bicycle, Mrs. Bentley regarded me with girl-like shyness from the corner of her eyes. If she was at all aware of the goings on at High Hearth or held any reservations over my lineage, she did not make it known. Her gaze only left me when one of the dogs whined, impatient at yet another delay. I thought to say something to reassure her of their gentle nature, lest she was like her husband, but before I could, she pointed to them with a delighted gasp, her timidity given way to captivation.

"May I?'

"Of course," I said, pleased at both her glee and forethought to seek permission before going to them. I snapped my fingers, calling my pair down from the cart.

Mr. Bentley returned to his wife's face buried in Cerberus' fur.

"Tillie!"

"Oh, they're wonderful. Simply wonderful!" she said while the dogs crowded close, nosing for their fair share of attention. "Come pet them, Crawford."

His moustache twitched. "No, I'm quite alright, thank you. Come away now, my dear, we must let Mrs. Fellowes be on her way."

After another series of hearty strokes, she thanked me and moved aside to let Mr. Bentley wheel the bicycle forward.

He held fast to one handlebar as I took the other, and when I looked to him in question, I was met with a deep set frown.

"Are you certain you wish to go alone?" he asked.

I glanced past him to his wife, then back. "Now more than ever. And I told you already, I shan't be alone."

He conceded with a reluctant nod. "Be safe, Mrs. Fel--" He paused and released the bicycle fully into my possession. "Eudora."

I smiled, and hoped with all my heart what I said next would not be the last I spoke to Mr. Crawford Bentley. "Thank you. Truly. I will call upon you again once I've seen this through."

"I will look forward to it."

I mounted the bicycle with a repeated thanks to Mrs. Bentley, who, to her husband's chagrin, requested I visit again with the hounds at my leisure.

"It is a peculiar hour to be making such a trip," she observed fretfully. "Do you know the way back to High Hearth? Will you be alright in the dark?"

"Yes," I said, my smile grave. "I do not fear the darkness."

***

Once outside the village, the road to High Hearth stretched long before me. The night sky was blessedly clear, and it was by the moon's pale cast that myself and my pair crossed into the countryside.

Lonesome winds rolled down hillsides and moaned through shallow valleys. How small I felt, surrounded by so much emptiness. How large the night. I pedaled as if the shadows themselves were in pursuit, and Black Shuck and Cerberus trotted merrily alongside me, glad for the extended excursion after so much stillness.

We carried on through the dark, the sole passengers upon that blackened path.

***

There lies a danger in such solitude, especially accompanied by so mindless a task as cycling. Stray thoughts are allowed to wander, to mingle, to take root and blossom into fully-formed ideas. As I rode, all the tiny resentments born from the repeated slights I'd been made to endure began to merge into a knotted and thorned thing.

I had come to High Hearth with the hopes of leaving speculation behind. The endless guesses and gossip as to who I was and the life I led. All I had wanted was a chance at peace.

Instead, I had been forced to adopt my great-aunt's mantle.

And now, because of it, without having spoken a single word to me, I was labeled a pariah, shunned and shamed for no greater crime than accepting an inheritance.

I had signed only for a house and her accounts, but in doing so, I had unwittingly taken on so much more.

A reputation unearned.

Old hurts, both inflicted and received, but neither by my hand.

Spectres of loved ones who had never lived in my heart.

All of these ghosts, left to me.

Always had I attempted to bear the misunderstandings and petty judgements with grace and good humour, but those had been built on my own behaviours. These that had been most recently laid upon me were not, and they stuck like thistles, poking and pricking at my patience.

Why should I be made a leprous outcast in her name?

Why should I be made to suffer?

To be a curious case, even a distasteful one, was one thing, but it was a different matter entirely to be so reviled for someone else's sins.

The bicycle's wheels churned hard over dirt as my anger turned to fuel and the desolate landscape sped by with the hounds bounding after.

***

Late was the hour of our arrival. High Hearth stood as a grand silhouette against the sky, its spires and peaks piercing upward and made all the more imposing by the night. The sight of it sent waves of cold washing down my back, but they did not, could not, run deep enough to extinguish the firestorm within.

The study key, tucked into the confines of my bodice, pressed hard against my chest.

My frantic pedalling slowed as we turned down the long drive, not from hesitation, but so that I could prepare myself for the encounter that was surely to come. I still did not know how I might confront Emmeline or what awaited me within that guarded room, but I armoured myself in prayer, trusting I would find a way to prevail.

I had to, if I wanted to be able to enter that house.

But as we neared, a figure, long-limbed, distended flesh white as fishbelly, scuttled from the cover of dark and hauled itself on to the drive in front of us. The air swelled with the stink of brine and spoilage.

"*Emmeliiiine.*"

The dogs leapt forward, placing themselves between me and the animated remains of my great-uncle, their fur raised from nose to tail and lips curled in terrible promise should he come closer.

"*Emmeliiiine.*"

Over the fearsome snarls, I heard him again, hissing her name as if it were mine.

"*Emmeliiiine.*"

Certainly his hideous visage did frighten me, the stark unnaturalness of it in conflict with my Godly soul, but even more than that, I was furious to such a degree that it surprised me, and despite my dread, a mounting voice demanded, *How dare he?*

How dare he place himself before me and call me by *her* name?

How dare he continue this trend of abuse, to look upon my face and see only her?

The anger that had carried me at so fast a clip blazed all the brighter, and I alighted from the bicycle, letting it tip, unnoticed, to the ground.

"Sit," I roared, and immediately my pair responded, startled into silence by my eruption. "Stay."

I stalked past them, fists balled tight at my sides. My breath came in shallow bursts, knees weakening with each step, but still I closed in on my great-uncle, whose twisted form shambled eagerly forward, until we two stood so close the stink of him threatened to strangle all of my faculties.

He gurgled, but with what emotion, I could not tell, and extended both arms, their flesh sloughed off at points along their gangling lengths to reveal bone and sinew beneath, toward me.

"I am *not* Emmeline," I screamed at him, and to everyone who refused to separate us.

He gnashed his broken teeth, bulging eyes rolling in their rotten sockets, and his fingers, cold and slimy as seaweed, curled around my forearms.

I tore my head away as he leaned in, his fetid breath a miasma upon my cheek, and heard my hounds' violent charge.

"Stay!" I commanded loudly, though my voice shook, and was rewarded with their slowing steps. They cried in unison, ever obedient even as it opposed their duty to defend.

"Whatever she has done to you," I spoke now to my great-uncle through clenched teeth, "however she has wronged you, I will not allow you to hold *me* responsible."

His grip tightened and he exhaled malodorous fumes upon my face.

I made myself look fully upon him, eyes narrowed into unwilling slits. "I am told you were a good man. A good husband. Look, *look*, and know I am not your wife," I said, my voice nearly failing me. "Emmeline is dead. I'm not her. I am Eudora, and you *will* recognize me as such."

His head cocked to the side in a series of twitches. There was hesitancy in the motion. His clouded gaze searched my features, flicking back and forth with increasing agitation. I shuddered as he lifted his fingers to my face, more so when he laid them across my cheek, stroking it with their spongey tips. With each repeated touch, a burbling grew in his throat, and when his mouth opened next, it was to emit a low, anguished groan.

The hounds growled and pawed at the ground as my great-uncle's hands slipped away and he teetered backwards.

"*Emmeliiiine*," he whimpered, and his heartbreak turned into a howling wail. "*Emmeliiiine*!"

He crumpled, clawing at himself, raking deep lines through his putrid flesh, and thrashing his torment into the earth. With tortured cries, he dragged himself from the drive and staggered once more into the dark, and after him trailed his miserable laments for Emmeline.

I swayed dangerously, hands pressed hard to my mouth to keep from screaming. The stink of him still clung to me and it made my gorge rise. I thought I might topple, sick and screaming, and feared that if I did, I would never stop.

It was my pair, as always, that returned me to my senses. Their gentle nudges and soft whines drew me outward, until my trembling ceased and I could breathe again. I stooped to cup their faces and kiss their foreheads, my tears of fright and gratitude wetting their fur.

"Thank you," I murmured to them and they wagged their tails. Of all the angels God had ever created, dogs were surely His greatest work.

After drying my eyes, I turned again to the house. It loomed over me, staring me down from its every window, all of them her eyes, already watching me. But I could not allow myself to be deterred. Not when I was so close to putting things to rest.

Let her watch.

Standing firm, I made the sign of the cross over my person and finished the journey to the front door with Black Shuck and Cerberus following faithfully behind. It practically leapt open at the lightest touch upon its handle.

I took a deep, slow breath, and stepped inside.

I had hardly made it across the threshold when the door slammed shut behind me, separating me from my pair and plunging me alone into the pitch black of High Hearth.

Chapter Sixteen

I fumbled for the doorknob, knowing full well before I found it that it would not turn. From the other side, my pair bayed and clawed as if they meant to burrow through its thick wood. I spun to face the front hall, back pinned to the door, and surveyed the darkness, impenetrable to my eyes.

The very air seemed to hum with lightning electricity, circling and swirling like a dense, weighted fog I could not see. It smelled of iron and tasted of blood. There was fury in it. I tried to breathe as little of it as I could for every inhale was an invitation for that cloud to turn to panic inside me.

There's nothing so valuable as the ability to think during troubled times, my parents' joined voices pushed back the creeping terror.

Think.

Think.

Think!

I had entered this house with a singular focus, and I honed all of my buzzing thoughts once more upon it, using it as the leverage I needed to make myself proceed.

I would uncover the secrets she harboured even in death.

I would see her undone.

Picturing the entryway as if it were daytime, I oriented myself in the direction of the study door and took a trepidatious step forward, hands held out in front of me like a child just learning to walk.

I had gone no more than a few, tiny steps when something rolled loudly across the floor from the direction of the parlour and came to rest against my foot.

I rounded my whole body toward it, arms waving wildly in an effort to ward off any attempts at attack. High Hearth's consistent thrumming heightened and intensified, the air swelling with a squall waiting to be unleashed, but remained otherwise unmoved, no assailant striking from its depths.

Yet.

She was waiting. I could feel it.

My fear fed her, allowing her to grow in strength as mine diminished, and grow she was. The walls veritably shook with it, the floorboards quavering. With the patience of a stalking tigress, she was observing, seeking out that opportune moment when she would be at the peak of her prowess.

I doubted very much she would be wasting energy by throwing things harmlessly at my feet. What, then, could it be?

Crouching with cautious slowness, I groped along the floor beside my boot until I came into contact with the item that had rolled to me. Smooth and slender, waxy, and beside it, a smaller wooden stick with rounded head.

I plucked both candle and match up with a softly uttered cry and peered sightlessly at the parlour.

"Morwen."

The match caught with a hard strike against the bottom of my boot and I lit the wick.

And in the candlelight, High Hearth came alive.

Phantom footsteps hastened from the kitchen, accompanied by the long shadow of a feminine figure that flickered with the candle's flame along the wall. That it came with no sense of impending danger, I recognized it as another memory resurfaced by the emotional surge, and followed the shadow's progress with the candle. It had almost reached the stairwell when a second set of steps, calmer, more deliberate, followed from the kitchen.

"Mrs. Bell."

Both the shadow-woman and myself became paralyzed by the voice, a woman's, albeit deep, cold and commanding, even while so calm.

"Yes, Lady Parsings?" The dark stand-in for a much younger Mrs. Bell made a poor show at matching her mistress' tone, her voice too high and reedy to be anything but suspect.

"You were in the garden just now, weren't you?"

"Why, no, Lady Parsings," Mrs. Bell lied with all the skill of a butcher who'd suddenly found himself in the ballet. "I was...I…"

"You saw."

There was no change in Emmeline's intonation, no accusation. Only certainty, and it was coloured with threat. Mrs. Bell's shadow fell prostrate, her hands clasped in pleading and raised toward the empty space before her.

"I will never tell a soul," she said. "May the good Lord strike me down should I even attempt to! I beg of you, my lady; please do not send me away."

The pause that followed was long and heavy, but when Emmeline deigned to speak again, her voice was softened by surprise. "You wish to remain? Even after..."

"I know the pains he put upon you, my lady. You did what you must to be free."

"You...do not think me a monster?"

"No," Mrs. Bell's shadow answered emphatically. "Is the prisoner who breaks unjust chains a monster?"

The shadow manoeuvred to its feet as if lifted by a second pair of hands.

"We two truly are of the same soul." Emotion, naked and intense, resonated in Emmeline's words, and she was unable to immediately continue. When she did, she had again adopted the cooler airs of control. "There is nothing to stand between us now. Send away for the girl. Bring my Thaddeus home."

So Mrs. Bell had known all along the nature of her employer, I thought as the shadow faded.

The front door creaked open behind me.

When I turned eagerly toward it, however, it was not to be reunited with my pair, who continued to cry havoc from outside, but to face another memory that had started with that cruel sound.

"Come inside." The shadow of Mrs. Bell appeared on the wall beside the door, and after her came a smaller one, timid even in silhouette. "There you are. Now, present yourself to the lady."

Her gesture indicated Emmeline had been waiting in the entry hall to receive them.

The timid shadow fell into a deep curtsey, and when she spoke, it was with the valley lilt of the Welsh. "My lady."

Heels clicked across the floor, followed by the rustle of clothing and the girl's surprised gasp. Slowly, she encircled her arms, embracing a figure lost to me.

"Welcome, Morwen," my great-aunt's voice murmured tearfully. "Thaddeus. My Thaddeus."

In a burst of emotion so vivid that tears sprang, unbidden, to my eyes, a series of scenes played out simultaneously around me. Each recollection dripped raw with love and with loss, with hurt and betrayal. With such sharp anger my chest ached.

Morwen hugging close to my great-aunt's skirts while they ascended the stairs, Emmeline offering words of comfort to her ward.

Morwen's girlish giggle from the parlour while Emmeline attempted to repeat a lullaby in Welsh.

Emmeline speaking to the child as if she were her late son and begging Morwen to relay messages from the dead.

Was Thaddeus hurting?

No, he knew only peace in the Kingdom of God.

Was he happy?

Yes.

Did Thaddeus forgive her for failing him?

There was nothing to forgive. He loved his mother, then and always.

The mood of the memories shifted quickly, each shadow extinguishing until there was only one left, bathed in a dour aura.

The girl, Morwen, on her knees, head bowed and shoulders shaking.

"I cannot do this any longer." She sobbed. "You have been so good to me, Lady Parsings, but I…"

"What is it, child?" Emmeline's concern was gentle and motherly.

"I have wronged you," Morwen said, fragile with honesty. "Thaddeus has never spoken through me. No one has. It was all my doing. I didn't want to! I'm sorry. I'm sorry."

"No," Emmeline denied it fervently. "You couldn't. You knew things--"

"It was the scullery maid, Martha. She wrote to my minder, the man who brought me here, and told him things so I could tell them to you."

Emmeline again tried to silence the girl, shouting her rebuke, but still Morwen cried out her wicked truth, her shadow doubled over in remorseful bow.

"She took payment from him to send him information, and more again when you purchased me. She has been the one telling me of Thaddeus, not his spirit."

"Silence," Emmeline shrieked. Morwen's shadow jerked backwards and the girl gasped and gurgled, limbs flailing, small hands clawing at her neck. "Be quiet! No more, no more."

Morwen's struggling slowed, her choking breaths became fewer, and I wept as my great-aunt did over the child's final suffering moments.

A great hush filled the hall, until Mrs. Bell's shadow flickered into life from the direction of the kitchen.

"My lady, did you give Martha leave to go? She just ran out the servant's entrance as if-- what's happened? Morwen! Oh, sweet child."

Morwen's still form slumped to the floor.

"She deceived me." Emmeline's whisper was made of grief and wrath. "This wretch, her minder, Martha...they *all* deceived me."

"My lady…"

The echo of Emmeline's sobbing gradually stopped, and in its place, there was left only devastating rage.

"Find me another," she spat, her demand venom. "Bring me another who calls herself medium. Bring me all of them! And let all who prey on sorrow learn its meaning to their marrow."

The final memory took me to the parlour, where Mrs. Bell's shadow hovered by the mantle.

"There are whispers in the village, my lady."

"There are always whispers in the village, Mrs. Bell," Emmeline replied from the area of the sofa. Gone was any trace of affection or warmth, her affect flat and distant.

"The Irish lass was one thing," Mrs. Bell continued anxiously. "But the southern woman was another. She came from wealth. Her family is looking for her."

"They came with poison intent. I merely served it back to them."

"There's talk of the police. What if Martha returns and tells them what she saw?"

"Martha will never come back. She fled, knowing she was caught. To return would be having to admit her part. Let them talk."

"But the study…"

"What of it?"

"If they go in there--"

"They will not," my great-aunt said. "For too long I have allowed the will of others to dictate my life. No more; I refuse to live in fear any longer. High Hearth is mine and mine alone. If they wish to enter it, they will have to wait until I am dead."

"Lady Parsings--"

"That's quite enough, Mrs. Bell," Emmeline said sharply, before adding, "But for your sake, I will retire from this business. For now. After all, I am still not finished with our current guests."

As Mrs. Bell's memory bled away into the dark, a ragged whimper sounded from the parlour’s far corner.

"Morwen?"

I turned, candle lifted, and caught in its glow, a sallow-faced spectre hurtled toward me.

Chapter Seventeen

Fingers closed like shackles around my wrists. The cold of them burned through my clothing, sapping my strength and numbing me to my elbows. The candle tipped, nearly slipping from my unfeeling extremities.

In the crooked light, her face was gaunt and wan behind lengths of hanging hair. Large eyes were rimmed in heavy black, her lips tinted blue, and, 'round her slender neck, a circle of dark bruises. Emmeline's eternal touch. That close, it was impossible not to be struck by her youth, her features still soft with lost childhood.

So young.

Too young for the pain and terror cut into her every expression.

"Morwen." The word came out in a winter's mist.

Her grip tightened in a desperate insistence emphasized by her pleading gaze. "*Go,*" the girl rasped, grimacing with the effort.

"I cannot," I said, though her frozen touch made the act difficult.

"*Go,*" she repeated, spasms of agitation rippling up her body. "*Hide. She's...coming...*"

"I know." I pried myself away, firm, but gentle, and was grateful for the immediate warmth that returned to my arms. "But I will stop her; I promise you."

Morwen flung her head back and forth with a guttural sob. "*Can't...can't...*"

"I must try!"

"*She's...coming...Hide!*"

The girl spun away with a pitiful cry and melted once more into High Hearth's shadows.

Morwen's fright was a dangerous contagion, bringing me a second's pause. If the dead had such cause to be afraid, then I, still living, had even greater reason to fear my great-aunt. She had proven time and again that the taking of a life was of little consequence to her. How much more depraved might death have made her, when all that remained was the hateful bitterness of a woman betrayed?

The longer I procrastinated, the more certain I was to find out.

There was nothing bold or brave in my scurry to the study door. Aside from the baying of my pair from outside, a profound silence had fallen over the house, like a bated breath waiting to turn to a scream. I checked repeatedly all around, expecting at any moment that Emmeline would appear at my side, and moved with clumsy, nervous haste. I felt as a thief, stealing through my own home with my back against the wall.

Before the door, I fumbled to pull the key from my bodice and lowered it to insert it into the lock.

It turned with a heavy *click*, and I twisted the knob, pulling fast to open it before my frayed nerves abandoned me, but not yet entering.

Within, hanging herbs and bones, scattered feathers and hardbound books, arcane symbols drawn upon the walls in varying degrees of frenzy. At the centre, a round table draped in lace.

And upon it, sitting in a circle of half-melted candles, a pair of skulls leered at a chair placed in front of them.

Nothing was so shocking, however, as the figure sprawled across the floor.

The vicar, Mr. Kenzie, lay on his side, facing away from me. An ugly wound gaped across the back of his skull, like a bloodied second mouth rimmed in dried red. He did not react to my entrance and from where I stood, I could not detect even a subtle rise and fall of his chest.

But he had gone; I had heard the door slam shut after him!

No, I realized with sinking dread. Not *the* door. *A* door.

This door.

My assumption had been that he had fled, but Emmeline had not allowed that. She had set upon him then trapped him here, in the one room beyond my reach.

Perhaps it had been that very burst of energy used to injure and ensnare the vicar, and her subsequent attack on me in the washroom, that kept her so tame toward me now while she regained her strength.

As I readied myself to go into that room, rife with an atmosphere befouled, fingertips appeared between the floorboards. Jagged-edged nails clawed and pulled as if their owners were surfacing upward from a hole.

Or shallow grave.

The first to emerge from the floor was a petite woman, black of hair, wide eyes glittering like sapphires in the candle light. Hers was the simple dress of a peasant, torn and caked in filth. She gripped her matted curls in double fists, whole body twitching and rocking. Beside her, a more stately figure, in an equally unkempt but properly tailored gown. Strands of her brunette hair flew free from their loose pins. She hugged her midsection, curled fingers digging into her sides, as convulsive as the other, and regarded me from behind cracked spectacles.

Bile and blood dripped from their mouths and nostrils, slathered their chin in streaks of ichor, stained their clothing fronts.

Their lips moved as if attempting to speak, but all that came out was unintelligible, throaty mewls marked by anguish.

The shorter of the two started toward me, her gait dragging and pained, and it was as she drew nearer I saw the raw stump of her tongue shorn down almost to its root. She made it within arm's length, stopping just short of a thick line of crystalline white spread across the threshold.

All at once, the spectral women sank back between the floorboards with gargled shouts, my candle was snuffed out, and I was pitched violently backward.

My head cracked hard against the wall, filling the sudden dark with bright spots. The force of the impact stole the air from my lungs and I went to my knees, gasping. Outside, the hounds beat upon the door with a new and terrible ferociousness that seemed so far from me.

A hand, cold and unforgiving as carved ice, closed in my hair, yanking hard to pull me across the floor. I shouted, both in shock and at the tearing of my tender scalp, and tried to find purchase in the floorboards to hinder further progress. I only succeeded in snapping my nail from its bed, drawing another injured cry from my lips. At the sound, I was flung again, and this time came to land amongst the scattered ruins of the tower I'd erected before the study door on my second night in High Hearth.

The porcelain and china I had placed as breakable warnings shattered beneath me, and their shards bit into my palms, splayed outward in weak attempt to catch myself. A weight sprang upon my back, pinning me down and pressing against the back of my head until my cheek raked against the cruel edges of broken things.

"*It's mine.*" Her voice was malice. Resentment. Contempt.

I floundered to escape her, each move driving slivers and splinters deeper into my flesh. The ravaging screams flooding my ears, animalistic in their terror and hurt, could not have belonged to me. I was not capable of such sounds! And yet, my throat burned with them.

"*You will not take it from me!*"

She bore down harder, stealing my breath, silencing my screams, and in their absence, the snap of my rib giving way came all the louder.

The front door shuddered. My pair threw themselves upon it with wild exuberance, their barking a maelstrom. Such was their savagery that Emmeline, so afraid of the canine kind, flickered, her weight vanishing.

"Cerberus," I called, or tried to. I could not tell if there had been any voice behind it at all. Tears fell in stinging drops over my damaged cheek. "Black Shuck!"

I crawled on hands and knees from the pile, leaving a trail of bloody prints, then staggered to my feet. The agonizing effort painted the edges of my vision in stark white. Fire blazed in my chest, roaring up and down my side, each breath fanning it to new heights. The door to my hounds seemed an eternity away, the span of the hallway an impossible trek through the gloom. I shuffled toward it anyway, thinking only of the dogs, of escape.

I made it to the parlour entrance, when a great gust hurled me sidelong into the room and sent me crashing against the piano and into the boxes beneath it.

I could not scream then, only lay there and wheeze.

The same footsteps from the memory, deliberate in their slowness, began their prowling approach from the hall, and as they grew closer, despair came with them.

How wholly unprepared I had been. How arrogant to think I could have done this alone. I had doubted her, believed too much in myself, and let my proud independence get the best of me.

What recourse had I now?

"Morwen," I could do no more than whisper. "Please. Help me."

"*Coward*," Emmeline said without inflection, and I did not know if she meant me or the girl.

Morwen did not appear, but a small fire, dim and weak, took light in the hearth. Emmeline hissed, and in its glow, I finally saw the woman. Mottled flesh stretched thin over bones, her eyes sunk deep into her skull. She was old and young at once, a creature that existed outside of time, and wore a gown styled for mourning, high necked and long, but instead of black, it was coloured a deep, dark red.

To look upon her was to see hatred wrapped in almost-human form.

But it was not Emmeline that Morwen wanted me to see.

As I turned 'round, trying to move further beneath the piano for some kind of protective barrier, I noticed one of the hat boxes had fallen over, spilling its contents. Old photographs in gilded frames.

And on top, one of a small boy in a dark suit with half-hooded eyes.

With great strain, I reached for it and thrust it upward as Emmeline closed in. The sight of it, as I had hoped, brought her to a jarring halt. Her expression wavered, granting me the courage I so dearly needed.

"Look at Thaddeus, Emmeline," I said with as much force as I could muster. Each word was the tip of a blade dragging up my torso, but I persisted, stilted though my speech was. "Look at your son. Tell me if this is who he'd want you to have become in his absence. Would he know you now, were you to meet again?"

I slid the frame across the floor to her, where it came to rest at her feet.

Emmeline tilted her head downward, hiding her face from me, and stared at the photograph.

Bolstered by her prolonged study, I sought to appeal further to her maternal grief. "He--"

"*--is dead,*" Emmeline finished callously, and she lifted one foot to bring it down hard upon the picture. "*And no one will use him against me again.*"

She crouched, and when again she stood, it was with a long shard of the frame's glass clutched in her hand.

I did not see her spring. One moment she stood feet away, the next she was upon me, and the glass was buried deep into my shoulder. I howled, a sound echoed from my distant pair, and Emmeline extracted the piece with a vicious upward tug.

As she readied it again, this time aiming more directly toward my pounding heart, a small voice sang from the shadows in a shaking attempt to soothe Emmeline's rage.

Huna blentyn ar fy mynwes,
Clyd a chynnes ydyw hon;
Breichiau mam sy'n dyn am danat,
Cariad mam sy dan fy mron...

Emmeline's maddened screech put an end to Morwen's song, and in a blink, my great-aunt had crossed to the corner of the room. The girl materialized unwillingly, cowering before her.

"*Devil's child,*" Emmeline said, and Morwen began to gasp and sputter as if the verbal barb were winding itself in a noose around her neck. "*Lying wretch!*"

Morwen grasped at her throat, eyes bulging, and fell back against the wall, trying to draw breath she should have no longer needed. The suffering of her final moments continued on, but this time, there would be no end until Emmeline decreed it. The girl staggered about in terrified torment.

Her eyes locked on mine, and in their tear-filled depths, I saw only suffering.

Hide, she had urged me, knowing the dangerous creature my great-aunt had become.

I had not listened, and in my hubris, I had put the both of us in peril.

This child, used in life, brutally and unfairly punished in death, had seen how dire my circumstance had become and chose to step forth, making herself known and taking Emmeline's wrath from me at a most crucial moment.

She who had been failed by all, even me, remained uncorrupted.

An innocent.

I used the piano to leverage myself to my feet. Doing so ignited every inch of my body, but I kept my focus in Morwen, who had collapsed to the floor.

"Leave her be." Mine was not the heroine's shout, but a breathless, uneven whisper.

Emmeline regarded me cooly from over her shoulder while Morwen writhed at her feet.

"Stop this!"

Morwen gaped soundlessly.

"Do you have no pity in you?" I croaked, provoking her with a name she had feared Mrs. Bell would give her. "Murderer. Monster!"

I had touched Emmeline's exposed nerve. Morwen was released from her cursed effect with a great gasp, shrinking instantly back into shadow, while my great-aunt whirled on me. Another gust, like the one that had knocked me into the parlour, but this time I managed to remain upright, both with the help of the piano and, I suspected, Emmeline's own weakening.

"I know the world was unkind to you," I laboured to say. "That you longed for a life different than the one you led. I am like you, made to live always as an outsider. I understand. But you have repaid hurt with hurt, and it cannot continue, Emmeline!"

She was at my throat, lifting me until I was suspended in the air by only her hands, frigid and suffocating.

"*You understand nothing.*"

My struggling was futile against the steel of Emmeline's grip. I could feel myself slipping further and further away even as my body continued its fight. The pain was unbearable, but the darkness beckoning from all around promised such sweet relief.

Sounds were distorted. Muddied. None made sense.

My sight was shrinking to a tunnel walled in white.

Emmelinc's smile was hungry and wicked.

So intent was she on watching my life ebb that the small figure cloaked in shadow escaped from the parlour unnoticed. I followed its progress with only the most vague sense I was doing so at all.

There was a sound in the hallway. A lock turning, perhaps.

Morwen's escaping.

The thought was warm, like a final smouldering ember on the verge of extinguishment.

There followed such a thunder that all of High Hearth shook with its coming, and in the weak glow of the hearth, fangs gleamed from the parlour’s doorway.

Black Shuck and Cerberus, shoulder to shoulder and snarling, as fearsome as their namesakes.

My pair leapt forward, Black Shuck launching himself over the sofa, Cerberus flanking from behind it. Emmeline's hands were gone from around my neck and I fell hard while the room spun in a cacophony of shrieking and growling. The hounds had chased Emmeline to the wall, where she attempted to flicker out of sight, but a pair of arms appeared to wrap tight around her waist.

Morwen clung to my great-aunt and together they turned to translucent mist, resolidified, and glimmered again.

Between her frenzied need to escape the dogs and Morwen's resistance, Emmeline's focus was broken, and she could only lead the girl to and fro in a panic-stricken dance met with snapping teeth at every turn.

From the midst of the chaos, Morwen shouted a single word.

"*Salt!*"

Salt.

What did that mean?

My thoughts were glacial, hardly connecting, until Morwen managed to add, "*Door!*"

The image of a thick, crystalline line of white surfaced. I'd seen that, hadn't I? Yes, only recently. In the study. It had repelled one of the women, keeping her trapped within.

Salt. Door.

Salt. Door.

There was nothing in my mind beyond that. No room for more. Only those two phrases, repeated with each staggering step to the kitchen and into the pantry, where I located the burlap sack from which the salt cellar was filled.

It weighed heavy as stone to my injured senses and I had to pull it, little by little, after me as I made my way back to the parlour.

Black Shuck and Cerberus maintained their vicious guard and still Morwen clung to Emmeline, who hissed and cursed and screamed, but could not escape the three of them.

Hardly able to remain upright, I sank to my knees and used my fast-dwindling strength to pour a line of white, thicker than the one in the study, halfway across the threshold.

"Morwen," I said weakly.

Her head jerked toward me, and understanding dawned upon her features when she saw what I had done.

I would not trap the girl in there with Emmeline.

We nodded to one another, and as soon as Morwen released Emmeline, I inhaled as deep as my wounded ribs would allow and called for the dogs.

My pair turned at my command and bounded toward me.

Morwan vanished, only to suddenly be at my side.

Emmeline realized, seconds too late, that she had been abandoned and, likewise, flickered from view.

But by then I had completed the line of salt, and when she reappeared, it was still on the other side of the barrier, sealed within the parlour.

With great difficulty, I hobbled upright, and slammed the door against her howling rage.

It was only a temporary hold, I knew, but it would have to be enough for the time being.

My consciousness was a tenuous thing, becoming more difficult each second to hold on to, but there was one thing yet to do.

With my pair trailing close as worried nursemaids, I made my way to the study and wiped a hand through the salt, upsetting the line.

I did not see them again, but felt the chill breeze of the two women fleeing past to freedom.

So done, I lowered myself against the wall and sat with legs splayed in front of me. Black Shuck and Cerberus nuzzled close, whining, and it was with their beloved faces filling my vision that I was finally able to close my eyes and sleep.

Epilogue

Mr. Bentley and his wife discovered me the following morning, when, upon Mrs. Bentley's insistence, they came to High Hearth to ensure I'd made the return journey without incident.

They had spotted me from the open front door, and discovered the vicar, barely clinging to life, moments later. Together they took us from the house and brought us, along with my hounds, to the village for treatment.

After he had healed, Mr. Kenzie claimed to have no recollection of High Hearth beyond being aware he'd visited me. That he'd caused my great-aunt's lingering spirit offense, been attacked, and thrown (for that was how I imagined Emmeline had placed him in the room without entering herself) into the study was lost to him. It was decided he must have crossed the same vagabonds who had waylaid me, as we were both said to have been found at the roadside.

That was what the Bentleys propagated throughout the village, anyway.

Mr. Kenzie never attempted a repeat visit.

Mrs. Bentley herself oversaw my recovery, and myself and my pair remained in their home for nearly a month, for which I was both immensely grateful and guilt-laden. Mr.

Bentley had a newfound appreciation for his office during that time, although I did sometimes witness him handing off scraps to the dogs after dinner when he thought no one would notice.

It was a peaceful time, and I was reminded of my childhood home, full of warmth and kinship and love.

But I could not remain. High Hearth loomed always.

I did not allow the Bentleys to accompany me back, hiring instead a gig to take me. I promised I would have them as guests once I determined it safe.

There is still much work to be done.

Hurt lives in High Hearth.

The kind of hurt that doesn't go away with prettied words and empty gestures. Staining its grounds, tainting its foundation, rooting itself deep.

Emmeline remains, tied to the place by chains forged in acrimony. I found her diaries, detailing her descent into the occult. How her fury had accidentally trapped Morwen, then her active practice captured the following two in the study with the intent of returning their inflicted torment tenfold.

There had been more mediums, far and away from her home, who she harmed during her travels, giving them poisoned goods they would use long after she'd gone.

People talked, however, and the name Emmeline Parsings became as poisoned as her gifts.

As age and a shrinking world, wiser to her misdeeds, prevented her from leaving home, she'd filled her house with things. Although never articulated, I felt a hunger in her writing, a desire for control she never felt she had, even when sitting before her victims' skulls, taunting their spirits, and from this spawned her habit of collection.

Never satisfied, never fulfilled, she died in her bed, alone, save for her loyal housekeeper, who would keep her secrets even after death, and all her empty, gathered things.

I have had to become a student of my great-aunt, using her own diaries to keep her contained. Salt, iron, runes, and arcane writings. I have learned of them all.

But not to harm.

Despite all she has done, my desire is to heal, and I am aided by my faithful pair, ever at my side, and Morwen, who has chosen to stay.

She saw goodness in Emmeline once. She believes it's there still.

We take turns sitting outside the parlour, spending time with her, talking to her, trying to remind her of the woman who had been capable of loving so deeply she would stand before the gates of Hell if it meant seeing her son again.

It is long and it is slow.

But the wounds were dealt long and they were dealt slow.

Morwen, the orphan who was sold by her parents and made to perform, only to be sold again, understands more than a child should.

And I, in all my privilege, have some measure of insight into living outside of a society that would rather see me broken.

Were it not for my parents' support, perhaps I would have become like her.

Perhaps that is why I stay.

Because to run would accomplish nothing. It would leave only another wound, another betrayal, another abandonment. If not for Emmeline, a complicated casualty, then for Morwen.

I cannot say if the scars of High Hearth will ever truly heal, and I cannot know if my great-aunt is truly redeemable. I have reason to believe our work is not without hope, however. I have not seen her husband roaming the grounds in some time, leading me to believe he is beyond her influence now.

It is a start, at least.

My great-aunt and I are alike in many ways. Our self-reliance, forward thinking, the simple, shared wish to dictate our own life paths.

But we differ, too, in a fundamental way.

I will not repay hurt with hurt.

I will end this cycle and put to rest her ghosts.

And I will remain in High Hearth, my home, where I am needed.

Where, at last, I belong.

Acknowledgements

Inheriting Her Ghosts would not have been possible without the tireless efforts of **Elle Turpitt**, who has been both a wonderful editor and friend these past few years. In addition to polishing the text and listening to me waffle on about ideas, Elle went above and beyond in assisting me with period research to ensure Eudora's world was as authentic as possible. She also provided a uniquely Welsh perspective that helped shape the character of Morwen, without whom High Hearth would have been a very different place. Thank you, Elle, for your endless support both on and off the page.

I would not be where I am as an author without **Olivia White**. She often works behind the scenes, going unnoticed and without thanks for everything she does (and trust me; it's a *lot*). So much of what I've been able to accomplish has been because of her pushing me forward, offering advice, and being a sounding board for ideas. It's rare to find someone you feel just *gets* you as a writer, and for me, that's been Olivia. Because of her, *Inheriting Her Ghosts* found an imprint to call home. Thank you for all you've done for me and my work.

Thank you to **David Cummings** for trusting in *IHG* enough to use it as a launching point for Sleepless Sanctuary Publishing and for all you do to support indie authors like me.

And finally, big thanks to **Erika Sanderson** for giving Eudora (and so many other characters of mine on The NoSleep Podcast) a voice.

~ Other Books by S.H. Cooper ~

The Corpse Garden

From Twisted Roots

The Festering Ones: Book 1 of The Ungodly Series

All That's Fair

All available on Amazon

~ About the Author ~

S.H. Cooper is a Florida based writer, which is really all you need to know about why horror might be her genre of choice. It's speculated she might have some relation to Florida Man, but so far she's remained tight lipped on the subject. *Inheriting Her Ghosts* is her sixth book and combines three of her favorite things: dogs, ghosts, and a remote mansion to run dramatically through whilst holding aloft a candelabra. While she's not British, she did visit the UK once years ago, which is almost the same thing, so writing a Victorian era gothic story set in the English countryside was an obvious choice. You can visit her online at www.authorshcooper.com or on Twitter (@MsPippinacious).